MASCARA

MASCARA

Death in the Tenderloin

By Ronald Tierney

In Appreciation

Thanks go to brothers Richard, Robbin and Ryan.
Also to Jovanne Reilly, David Anderson,
Dennis Gallagher and John Sullivan

Life, Death and Fog Books
968 Central Avenue
San Francisco, CA 94115

Email: rtierney@44sbcglobal.net
www.ronaldtierney.com

Book design: Dennis Gallagher and John Sullivan/visdesign.com

Library of Congress Cataloguing-in-Publication Data
Tierney, Ronald.
Mascara, Death in the Tenderloin/ Ronald Tierney—1st. ed.
p. cm.
ISBN: 978-0615493565

1. Private Investigators—California—San Francisco—Fiction. 2. Murder—Fiction.
3. Missing Person—Fiction 4. Detective and Mystery Stories. I. Title.

813.5'4-dc22

First Edition 2011

The Tenderloin *is a tough San Francisco neighborhood. It was even tougher in mid 1990s when this story begins. Drugs, prostitution, poverty combined to create a netherworld. A body found here or there on those streets wouldn't be met with surprise, but one of them would haunt the days and nights of a private detective's life, whose brief was as disorienting as the Tenderloin itself. This is also the beginning of a strange and enduring partnership.*

ONE

"MIGHT BE A good idea to tell somebody first," he said as he relaxed back in the beat-up upholstered chair.

No answer.

His voice seemed to hang on a precipice. Nearly gone. Faint. No bass, no treble. The sound of wind over tall grass. Lulling, friendly.

He was talking to the slender, naked being, framed by the doorway of the bathroom and backlit by the morning light from the window farther back in the narrow space.

He thought he should have known.

"It didn't seem to bother you last night."

He didn't know last night. He'd never know if he had somehow participated in the deception. Noah was a little drunk. And . . . well . . . things got out of hand quickly.

Noah had dressed. A white tee shirt. Old, pale jeans, the denim thin from years of wear. Yet they fit his lanky body perfectly. He was handsome, but probably hadn't always been. A close look at his face showed that acne raged at one time, leaving behind little pock marks that kept him from being pretty. His hair was wiry, blond. Eyes mostly gray. In the right light, though, one could see a hint of blue. He seemed real ordinary at first glance. On the second, the weathered good looks of a relaxed country boy came through.

Noah watched as Sasha ran a washcloth over small, firm breasts. He tried to guess whether Sasha was Asian or Latino. "I won't be long." After a short pause, Sasha continued. "So if this is your office, you probably have a wife back home, wondering where you are."

"This is home," Noah said.

1

"No wife?"

"No."

"No kids?"

"No."

"No shower?"

"I don't believe in bathing," Noah said.

Sasha came to the door smiling, leaned against the frame in a comically seductive stance — a beautiful, smooth and extraordinarily feminine body — spoiled for Noah, by a penis.

"So, are you really heterosexual?" Sasha asked.

"Probably."

"Probably? How old are you? Aren't you sure about what you like?"

"I'm not sure about much of anything," he said, realizing Sasha had taken him literally. Then what did he expect from someone who didn't know him, didn't have a chance to figure out he was a smart ass? Likely wouldn't either. He was pretty sure their paths would never cross again.

"So . . . I keep saying 'so' don't I? Anyway, do you like me?"

"You're okay."

"You want me to hurry up and get out of here, right?"

"No rush, but sometime this morning, maybe. Soon you know." He revised his terms. There was still too much morning left. "I have work to do." He hoped that was graceful enough and clear enough. As far as Noah knew he was totally heterosexual. And he wasn't likely to use Sasha's services in the next fifty or sixty years.

Sasha came over to him, knelt down, put his hands on Noah's knee. "Are you going to want to see me again?"

"One never knows about these things." He should have just said "no," he thought. Somehow he couldn't. A year or so ago — after some convoluted arguments, he'd concluded that seeing the occasional prostitute was not wrong. What he'd tried to convince himself of was that it didn't diminish him. An adult act. Convenience. A way to keep life simple. An honest business deal between two consenting adults. Now he'd spent the night with whatever Sasha was. A little too much drink, then things moving along before. . . .

"It's possible, then?" Sasha stood, a suggestion of a smile on his face. Then, getting no response, turned back toward the bathroom. "I guess not. Wait," the guest said, standing again in the doorway, tucking his penis between the smooth thighs, out of sight. Only a small patch of pubic hair visible. "This better?"

The breasts. The face. The body. Mighty convincing.

Noah didn't answer. It really wasn't better. It blurred any remaining distinctions between what you saw and what you got.

"You have a way of making coffee around here?" Sasha asked. Not getting an answer, Sasha shrugged. "Then I'll be good and leave."

Noah looked up.

"I promise," Sasha said, still amused.

"Coffee. I can handle coffee," Noah said. He didn't want to extend Sasha's stay. But what would a cup of coffee add? Fifteen minutes? He lied about having work to do. He just wanted to get this over with. His mind was working extra hard trying not to remember last night. He was happy that the details, whatever they were, were lost in the haziness of a hangover.

Sasha dressed while Noah made coffee.

"You live AND work in this place?" Sasha said, sliding the jeans over narrow hips and, after a gentle tuck, hiding all hint of the male gender.

"My world is very small," Noah said.

"Where does that door go? A closet?"

"Storage room."

"What do you store in there?"

"My entire estate. You ask a lot of questions."

Sasha turned, leaned over to slip on the high heels. So sensual, even from behind. Who wouldn't have been fooled?

"The sign outside says 'Tracker Investigations.'" Sasha straightened, turned back, tossed her head, black hair following seductively as intended.

"So it does," Noah said. The harsher, cold light came through the office window. Sasha wasn't sixteen, thank God. Holding back thirty, he thought, and doing a pretty good job at it.

"Your name Tracker?" Sasha still hadn't covered his or her breasts, apparently knowing what lingering vision to leave in Noah's brain.

"No. It was my partner's idea. The name."

"Sounds like a TV show." Sasha slid the sweater on. Only thing bare to the chilly morning now was the flat pecan-brown midriff, and a navel pierced and glittering with a small gold ring. "So where's your partner?"

"In a jar somewhere."

"Oh."

"Your mother shrink your sweater?" Noah asked. Unlike some of the tranny hustlers Noah had seen on the streets, Sasha didn't over play it. A tart, yes — hence the little navel nudity. But subtle with the make-up. Light on the attitude. Natural, he thought. Sasha's deception was masterful. Sober, in the morning, he might have figured it out. Drunk, at night, he didn't stand a chance.

Noah pulled the sheet, pillow and blanket from the brown vinyl sofa. It smelled of sleep and sex, the scents no doubt heightened by the heat of the radiator. He was surprised he slept. He was surprised. . . .

"Coffee's good," Sasha said, taking a sip and sitting on the bare vinyl. He used two hands to hold the large cup. Long, elegant fingers gathering warmth.

Noah stuffed the wadded bed linen in a corner behind a stack of books. He noticed Sasha taking in the environment.

What were Sasha's eyes taking in? The fact that the walls needed painting? Windows were dirty? That the vinyl on the sofa was ripped in several places and had been covered over with duct tape? The matching chair matched all too well. The desk was an old wooden thing with battle scars and one drawer missing. The hardwood floors had been scuffed raw. Bookcases lined one wall, shelves occupied by a few worn paperbacks. In a corner was a tiny, dented refrigerator. On top of that was a rusty hot plate with a frayed electrical cord. One stained, over-stuffed chair and another desk chair with a ripped seat, both of which he'd salvaged from the sidewalk, pretty much completed the inventory.

"Is it all right if I come by sometime?"

Noah didn't know what to say. Again, he'd been put on the spot. Perhaps he'd have to be firm. This could get out of hand quickly.

"A visit?" Sasha suggested in the silence.

"Wouldn't be a smart marketing decision, Sasha."

"What marketing?"

"I don't have a lot of money, as you can see," Noah said.

"I didn't ask for money," Sasha said. "Did I?"

4

"No, but…"

"I know. It was that time. That place." Sasha smiled. "I don't blame you. I work late. I go home that way. You pulled over. I didn't know you didn't know. You looked so lonely."

"You a saint?" Noah asked.

"No. It'd be a long time before a church took up for someone like me. You had a nice face. I was lonely too. So, is it all right if I drop by some time?"

"Why?"

"Maybe just to talk. About the weather. Sports, that kind of thing."

"You into sports?"

"No," Sasha said smiling. "But I can listen."

"I'm not much of a talker."

Sasha smiled.

"I don't care. Just want to stop by and. . . ." Sasha let the sentence trail off into oblivion.

"Yeah . . . sure." He wasn't sure why he agreed. No future in it. Hell, there wasn't much of a future in anything. He just found it difficult to be blunt. To hurt someone else who was just trying to scratch out an existence. On the other hand, if things kept going like this, he'd marry this boy or girl or whatever Sasha was before lunch just to keep from hurting his feelings. He didn't dislike her . . . him. Well, he thought to himself, it was a "him," wasn't it? No, the lines were definitely blurred. Weren't they all? "Now, I have some work. . . ."

"Oh, by the way," Sasha said at the door. "You're still heterosexual. All the way."

The fact of the matter is that Noah didn't have work. He didn't get very many job offers these days. In the last few years, he'd stayed afloat by picking up a few hours on stakeouts for insurance investigators, occasionally retrieving an automobile that was a little too expensive for the buyer's tastes, and every once in awhile tracking down the more harmless of the bail jumpers. Most of his jobs, sparse as they were, came by way of telephone from people with whom he had at least some vague acquaintance.

So, he was surprised when the second visitor in 24 hours arrived.

It was afternoon. Sasha's scent still lingered in the room, and into it walked a tall, fortyish woman who, judging by her clothes, had to be slumming. Noah couldn't tell Donna Karan from Gucci, but he could pretty much identify the league.

"And you are?" she asked.

"Noah."

"Noah. Good enough, I guess. I'm interviewing investigation firms."

"Is this a hobby?"

"A necessity, unfortunately. I had an appointment with Mr. Brinkman down the hall and saw your sign. While I was here. . . ."

"Brinkman. Me. Funny, you don't look like a K-Mart shopper to me."

"I don't want a high profile firm."

"Then you have come to the right place. We don't even have a low profile. I don't even cast a shadow."

"May I sit down."

"Sure," Noah stood, hands offering the vinyl sofa.

She sat precisely where Sasha sat. Noah looked for an Adam's apple.

"My name is Olympia Rawley."

Noah waited for her to continue. She didn't look like an "Olympia." His brain went from the brand of beer to mythology. Maybe the latter. She possessed something special. Something powerful. Authoritative. An older goddess type, but a goddess nonetheless. Diana of the Hunt.

She waited too, waited for the name to mean something to him.

"That's a start," he said. "I have your name so I know what to put on top of the invoice. What can I do for you?"

"Find my husband, Charles."

Charles Rawley did mean something. Noah didn't have to scour the gray matter for this one. Local boy on the Forbes 100 list. Multi-multi-multi-billionaire. Olympia Rawley *was* slumming.

"Now I'm really puzzled," Noah said. "You can afford somebody really good. Why are you even considering me . . . or Brinkman for that matter?"

"I'm not considering. I'm hiring you. Otherwise I wouldn't have told you my name. This has to be done with extreme discretion. Too many people involved in the larger firms."

"Pretty short interview. Which of my sterling qualifications did you pick up on?"

"It doesn't take me long to judge character."

"What if you're wrong? What if, and I say this only as the longest possible shot, I am a completely unreliable flake with very little real experience?"

"That's okay." She smiled.

"What if I call the local news and start talking?"

"I'd have you killed," she said.

"Maybe you ought to find someone else," Noah said. She had to be kidding, but it didn't sound like it.

"Too late. You already know."

"What about Brinkman?"

"Names didn't come up. And there's no need to bring them up with Mr. Brinkman or anyone else. Right?" She opened her bag, pulled out an envelope.

Noah nodded.

"Everything you need is in here. You are not to call me. You are not to contact me in any way. I'll contact you. You are in the phone book, right?"

"Don't look for anything flashy."

"No card?" she smiled.

"At the printers," he said — his line for the last ten years.

Noah started to open the envelope.

She put her hand on the envelope. "No need to do that now. I'm sure the advance is sufficient to get you started. I'll call you tomorrow."

There were questions. Dozens of them. But he was too stunned by the abruptness of the deal. He nodded, smiled faintly.

She left.

TWO

FIFTY ONE-HUNDRED-DOLLAR BILLS didn't take up much space in the 5x7 manila envelope. Also inside was a photograph of Charles Rawley — a head shot, the kind that runs in the business section of a newspaper. Another piece of paper, obviously run out on some sort of laser printer, listed some stark statistics.

```
Name: Charles William Rawley
Age: 55
Birthplace: Atlanta, Georgia
Residence: Hillsborough, California
Height: 5'9"
Weight: 153 lbs.
Eyes: Blue
Hair: Receding, salt and pepper
Distinguishing characteristics: pale scar on
right eyelid
Family: Olympia, wife
   David, son.
Occupation: Financier
```

Noah thought that perhaps "corporate raider" was a more appropriate designation for the kind of work the guy did. Not much to go on, except that someone with Rawley's kind of notoriety is hard to hide.

He should be happy. Work. He wasn't happy. Something was wrong. It all happened too quick. He knew too little. On the other hand, $5,000 stared him in the face. A week's grocery money for the Olympia Rawleys of the world. A few months of comfortable living for the likes of Noah Lang. And this was just an advance. More to come. He stuffed the envelope into the ripped upholstery of his desk chair and went down the hall to see Brinkman.

Brinkman's office was about the same size as his own. The furniture was about the same vintage. The difference was that Brinkman's depression era furnishings were clean, the furniture was in relatively good shape and he had "his girl" to welcome potential clients and get rid of unwanted visitors — bill collectors for example. Always a girl. Not a woman. Not a lady. Not a female person. His "girl." Quite often a different girl. He changed his receptionists more often than he changed his underwear.

Delores was the girl of the week, though much like the other girls. A little brassy, a little bosomy. Friendly. Underpaid. Possibly incompetent, but apparently willing to put up with Brinkman's shenanigans — for awhile anyway. Her little desk on the small side of Brinkman's glass partitioned office faced the door. Her smile contained more than a hint of flirtation.

The top of Brinkman's head could be seen behind a racing form. Harsh fluorescent lighting flashed on the surface as his head bowed deeper into the statistics.

Noah went past Delores — wasn't there a "Doreen" here once? — knocked on the glass. Brinkman jerked, looked pissed. Then smiled, waving Noah into the stuffy tobacco-smelling air.

"You send me a client, Barry?"

Barry laughed, coughed, laughed again. He looked like Nixon would have looked in a flat top. Barry picked up his cheap, dead cigar and brought it to stinking life with the strike of a wooden match.

A waft of sulfur.

"One crazy bitch, huh" he said, moving around Noah and closing the door. He shook his head. "She calls. Sets up an appointment. Won't give her name. Won't tell me what she's lookin' for. I agree. Shoulda told her to go take a flying fuck, but I agree. Look around. I gotta live. I gotta pay Doris."

"Delores. The sign says, 'Delores.'"

"All right. If you like."

"And you had a 'Doreen' once, didn't you?"

"Yeah? So what?"

"You should move on to the 'f's — hire a Felicia or Francine. Then you might not confuse them."

Brinkman looked at Noah like he was crazy. "Delores. She's got a litter of kids and a husband with a back problem. I tell her it's because he was born without a spine, but . . ."

"But you agreed to meet her?"

"Doris? Delores," he corrected himself angrily. He shook his head. Took a hit off the cigar. "Oh, yeah. The snooty broad. So I agree." Another hit. "Cause I'm an angel. Everybody deserves a chance even if they give me that mysterioso crap, you know what I mean?"

Noah nodded.

"She comes in here like she's the Queen of Monaco, don't tell me her name. Don't tell me nothing. She takes one look at me, shakes her head and acts as if she's just made this huge mistake, like she just walked into the men's toilet, and hauls her royal ass outta here."

"Why?"

"How the fuck do I know?" He took another puff on his cigar — a long draw. Comes back from smoker reverie and said with a cocky smile, "Methinks she didn't like the cut of my jib," his language slipping from street to stage affectation without warning.

"You cut your jib. Tough luck. Stitches?"

"She goes to you after stiffing me?"

Noah shrugs.

"What happened?"

"Pretty much the same thing. I don't think she liked my jib any better than yours." Noah felt justified in the lie. Brinkman had lied to him from time to time.

"Lord help us, Noah. Can't these snooty tight asses figure out from the neighborhood that this ain't Saks Fifth Avenue?"

"You didn't get her story?"

"I figure it's one of two things. She's got a husband who won't stay in his stall or she's got a gigolo she wants checked for priors. She's nice lookin', but no spring chicken. Because money is the succor of old age —and my guess is she's got plenty of succor — she probably wants to make sure she don't lose the golden goose."

"Yeah, probably. Thanks." Noah started to go, then stopped. "Oh, watch your metaphors."

Brinkman grinned. "You think somebody's out to heist 'em."

"Probably."

They both laughed.

In the corporate world, they call it "due diligence" — that is checking out the credentials and background of a person with whom you intend to do business. Noah hated looking a gift horse in the mouth, but Olympia Rawley's sudden appearance caught Noah off guard and her quick disappearance caught him napping. He hadn't asked the right questions. Double checking her story with Brinkman was only a tiny step in the verification process.

The public library was a cheap resource and would no doubt offer some further information on the matter of Olympia and her husband, Charles. He was sure volumes of facts, gossip and analyses existed on this man, one of the richest and most powerful men in America. Almost as important at the moment, was verifying Olympia. Surely pictures of Mrs. Rawley would be in abundance. Outside verification was better than asking his client for her I.D. After receiving $5,000, it would seem pretty unappreciative.

He hadn't been in the public library for years. In fact, it wasn't even the same public library. This one was clean, brightly lit and full of computers. His first reaction was "oops." His lack of knowledge of and interest in the world of high technology was one of the many reasons — lack of ambition having the most impact — he was sliding toward the absolute bottom of his profession.

He owned no shiny gadgets to record conversations from the changing molecular structure of windows 40 feet away. No infrared cameras to catch copulating couples in the darkness. No identity tracking from sophisticated search programs on the computer. Though he didn't consider himself young at 32, he was too fucking young to be a dinosaur, wasn't he? He knew the answer. And he didn't like it.

He looked through the biography section and found three books without the help of the plugged-in and apparently vastly superior, binary brains on tables throughout the rooms. One book was *The Samurai for the '80s*, written by some *Wall Street Journal* reporter. Both of the others were newer. *Quest* was written by Charles Rawley himself five years ago. "Charles Rawley" was in huge letters, larger than the title. Smaller and nearly hidden in the pattern of Rawley's tie was "with John Caldwell." The third book was two years old and was more promising. *Collateral Damage,* by James Morcham, suggested that the writer was not engaged in hero worship.

An Evelyn Wood course would have been helpful. Noah wasn't a patient person. He scanned as best he could, going through the *Samurai* book with great speed, noting special enemies and getting his first glimpse of a man completely void of sentimentality. This was a characteristic that served ambitious people well. The vagaries of human suffering were machete-cut from the paths to profit like so much undergrowth.

Quest turned out to be surprising. It was Rawley's own unsentimental look at his character. "Leaders are required to look out for the greater good." The question of whose greater good wasn't exactly answered, at least in the detective's quick scan. The book had pictures — dozens of them in a special middle section. None showed a wife — nor the son, for that matter. The only thing that set this version of Charles Rawley's life apart from the lives of all of the other corporate raiders, brutal downsizers and union slayers was that Rawley was now purporting to have a deeply "spiritual" side.

He often used the word, "purity," as something synonymous with "spirituality." What Rawley really meant was "clarity," Noah thought. Rawley believed he saw the world for what it was and acted in his own best interest. His gain was his reward. He was blessed because he was "pure." This was the way the world worked and for those who didn't get it? Tough.

Whatever gets you through the night, Noah thought.

"Quest" was the word Rawley used in the title because it was the search for purity and it was what he called his annual isolation from the world. He would take one month every year and disappear on this "quest." According to Rawley, the 30-day isolation could take place in a rain forest or a mountaintop or a desert. No one could reach him. His loved ones could die, or worse, he could lose market share in some new acquisition, and he wouldn't know until the quest was over. He believed that these retreats were the key to the purity it took to remain sharply in tune with the power that made him successful.

Charles Rawley's mantra was: Think clearly, act decisively.

Two books down, seven pages of scrawled notes and Noah's eyes were tired, his mind dulled and his stomach in turmoil. He hadn't eaten and it was now past 6 p.m. He hid *Collateral Damage* on a shelf of "Jacobean Drama," and went out into a familiar grayness. It had been constant since morning and gave the day a sense of not passing, of existence stalled.

Noah took comfort in the sludge of fast food. It didn't require thought. It merely satisfied the urges, as did his nightly drug of TV, with the meaninglessness of it all obliterated by cheap beer. Life had been like that. Even his escapades had been vanilla. Well, until last night. And that was a little too spicy for him.

Noah returned to the library. Back to the book on the "collateral damage" of Charles Rawley's corporate wars. He checked the index first for signs of an "Olympia Rawley." No such entry had been made. Two entries in the "Rawley" index showed female names. "Margaret" and "Ruth."

Ruth turned out to be Rawley's mother. But Margaret was his wife. He checked all three paltry passages referenced in the index. Margaret had been mentioned incidentally until the third reference when it was clear she was mentally ill and placed in an expensive sanitarium until she died. Her death was far too mysterious for the biographer's taste.

The only mention that Noah could find about his wife's death was, "Most people do not live, they just try to occupy their lives until they die. Margaret's last years weren't even occupied."

Noah would be hard pressed to disagree with the bitterly disgruntled author. Margaret's death was apparently inconsequential to the tycoon. He scanned the rest of the book, saw that it offered nothing new about Charles Rawley, though it stacked the awful evidence of his callous disregard for the rest of humanity higher and higher and presented corporations in general — and corporate raider Rawley in particular — as the Ghengis Khans of the 20th Century.

Two things troubled Noah as he closed the book and scooted if off to the farthest reaches of the building. The first was that he still had no verification of Olympia Rawley's identity. The second, a fuzzier concern, was a question. Wasn't it possible that Rawley was merely off on some retreat and Olympia Rawley, if she was Olympia Rawley, had some very important reason to contact him?

Noah Lang needed far more current information. *Time*, *Newsweek*, the *Journal*. He checked his watch. The library was closing in an hour. No time for the long, boring trudge through the periodical section.

The man behind the counter in the business area suggested Noah go up a few floors. There he would find a number of computers. "You (meaning Noah the techno idiot) should be able to find current information on the subject rather quickly."

THREE

THE DECISION TO look foolish didn't take him long to make. A few frustrating stabs in front of the screen got him nowhere.

"I'll give you ten bucks to help me with this," Noah told the 12-year-old boy sitting at the next computer.

"Ten bucks?" the kid asked. He was actually mulling this over. "You want me to find the porn sites?"

"No, Jesus!"

"I can. It's easy."

"No, listen. Whoa." Noah looked over at the kid's monitor, which had been skewed toward the wall forming a little private viewing booth. Tits in Technicolor greeted his inquiry. He felt foolish. Here he was with some pubescent gnome leading him into the world of computer porn. He didn't know whether it was disgusting or frightening. Then again, maybe he should listen or at least go back to Sexuality 101 where one could learn to identify the female of the species.

"No," Noah kept protesting. "You know you could be arrested for contributing to the delinquency of an idiot."

"The idiot being you."

"Yes," Noah admitted. "I need to get the latest information on some guy."

The kid scooted over, apparently not wanting to lose his own place on the Internet. "You know the guy's name?"

"Of course."

"Okay." The kid pulled the keyboard toward him. "The first thing we have to do is find a search engine."

"Whatever you say," Noah said.

"Name?"

"My name?"

"If that's who you want to look up."

Noah made a nasty face.

"Charles Rawley. R-A-W-L-E-Y."

"I know."

It could have been 'R-A-L-E-I-G-H,' like Raleigh, South Carolina."

"North Carolina," the kid said.

"No, it isn't."

"Yes, it is. North Carolina"

"Is not."

"Is too," Noah continued, but realizing he was probably wrong.

"Is not."

"Shut up," Noah said. "You want the ten dollars or not?"

"Twenty."

"We agreed on ten."

"Yes, but you're being difficult."

Noah was a difficult student. But he learned. He could now go to the library and do this himself. What he learned about Charles Rawley in the hour of Internet enlightenment wasn't much more than he already knew. Except that an on-line magazine had an article on Rawley that indicated he had married again. Recently. Unfortunately the acknowledgement, the life of the wife — an "Olympia" as it turned out — was to be kept private. No interviews with the woman. No photographs. This now mysterious woman wasn't the subject of the article — merely an interesting anecdote as the story of Rawley's increasing wealth and power unfolded.

The story hinted strongly that while Rawley was respected and despised as much as Microsoft's Bill Gates, Rawley's ruthlessness wasn't confined to the relatively polite world of collusion, price fixing and leveraged, if not downright hostile, takeovers. Rawley, not a guy who ever had a slide rule and a plastic pocket protector, was a threat in many more ways.

"Heroes and villains," Noah said as he left the library and searched for his car. The world has to have its drama. The journalists have to have a good story. Otherwise you don't sell Rice Krispies and nobody gets paid.

He checked the windshield of his little car for tickets. Fortunately he'd escaped the law this time. He got inside, chastising himself for such bad housecleaning. Coffee stained paper cups littered the floor on the passenger side. There was a scrunched Burger King bag that still emitted the smell of grease and meat in the seat.

What did it matter? The vehicle itself wasn't much of a looker. It was dented, scratched and bruised. The windshield was cracked. His little Alfa Romeo coupe should have been prestigious, but it was old, very old and battered. The black paint had faded. It had served him well. It was, in fact the only thing Noah got in the divorce settlement. Fitting, because all of his belongings — now in the storage room at the office — fit in the little car. Using the passenger seat, the back seat and the tiny trunk, Noah could cram his entire life into it and move on. Moving on was a constant theme and it didn't require making a decision and then actually doing it, he might have done it already.

He thought maybe he'd try to find the author of *Collateral Damage*. Someone who hates that much is likely to have kept track of his archenemy. Enemies were somewhat unreliable, but better sources than friends or frightened allies. Should be able to track him down. An uncommon name — Morcham — and he lived in the area according to the snippet of a bio on the book jacket.

No more investigation tonight. The library wore him out. He'd be less tired if he'd run five miles up a hill. As it turned out, neither mind nor body was ready to give up. Noah lay awake, troubled by thoughts of Olympia and perhaps even more by Sasha.

It was a dreamless sleep as far as Noah knew. The last thing he remembered was checking his Timex glow in the-dark watch and seeing that it was 4 a.m. The next thing he knew was the light penetrating his eyelids. The light came too soon. However it wasn't what dragged him into the real world. It was the knocking.

The first thing he did was check his watch. The big hand was on the eleven and the little one was nearing the nine. He sat up with a start. He didn't want to be groggy when Olympia Rawley called. The alleged

Olympia Rawley, he thought. The knocking was merely an irritant until a frightening thought came from nowhere and landed in his brain. What if Olympia changed her mind about the phone call and decided to make a second appearance?

"Who is it?"

"Me."

Who in the hell was "me?" he thought. Was that Olympia's voice? "Just a moment," he said, looking for his underwear — dressing quickly. He ran his hand through his hair, trying to gain full and clear consciousness. He grabbed the sheet, blanket and pillow in one grasp and tossed it into the storage room.

He went to the door — uncombed, disheveled and with morning breath — and opened it, hoping it wasn't the Rawley Goddess.

It wasn't. But his heart sank anyway. Noah wasn't prepared to deal with this — not as the first obstacle of the day.

Sasha stood there smiling, a lidded paper cup in each hand.

"Latte?"

"Uh. . . . Sasha. It's early. I. . . ."

"You need some coffee, I can tell." He stepped in. "You don't have a microwave do you?"

"No."

"I hope this is hot enough. You like Latte?"

"I'm kind of a regular guy," Noah said, trying to suggest that he liked his coffee as straight as his sex; but he'd already given in. He couldn't send Sasha away, though he suspected that would have been the smartest and perhaps, in the long run, kindest thing he could do. "Just a regular kind of guy."

"I know," Sasha said, making it sound like a criticism. "But that's why I like you. Try this. It's good. Some chocolate. Some cinnamon."

Noah took the cup, set it on the desk.

"Sasha."

"What?" he peeled off the lid to his coffee, licked the foam.

Noah wanted to say, "I work here. I've got to get to work. I'm not into transvestites." Instead, he said, "Thank you."

Sasha looked even more boyish today. No make up. Even so, he'd still take him for a her. The breasts. The mannerisms.

18

"I just stopped by to say 'hi.' Thank you for the other night."

"You don't have to do that."

"I wanted to." Sasha sat on the sofa. "You were nice, given the situation. A lot of guys. . . ." Sasha didn't finish the sentence.

"So . . . uh. . . ."

"Don't worry, I won't stay. You have to work."

"That's all right." Noah hoped that wasn't too encouraging. "Yeah, I have to work, but I have a few minutes."

The phone rang.

"Noah Lang," he said.

"Mr. Lang. This is your new client."

"Hello," Noah said, picking up quickly that she didn't want to mention names on the telephone.

"Are we set?"

"I have some questions."

"You do?"

"I haven't been able to . . . uh . . . verify.. . ." he exhaled. Nothing to do, but to do it. ". . . who you are."

"I see," she said coldly. "I pay you to do one thing and you decide you want to investigate me."

"It's important that I know who I'm working for."

"You have other questions?"

"Yes." He was hoping he didn't have to ask them now. Not just because he had a visitor, but because he had not thought about any of this since yesterday.

"Tonight, Mr. Lang, you board the last ferry to Tiburon. Take the one from the Ferry Building. Go to the top deck. The rear."

"The stern?"

"Yes. The stern," she conceded grudgingly. "Got it?"

"Listen, umm. . . ."

Click.

"You don't have a radio or anything?" Sasha asked.

"No. Just a TV."

"Don't you like to listen to music?"

"I haven't thought about it much lately." He looked at his watch.

"Should I go?"

Noah denied audibility to his "yes." Instead, he said, "No, just trying to figure out where I was in the day, that's all."

"You haven't touched your latte."

"Oh, yes. Yes." He pulled off the lid, took a sip.

"You have to have music in your life. What is your music?"

"I don't know what you mean," Noah said, sitting on the edge of the desk.

"The music that makes you feel like you. Classical? Blues?"

"I don't know. What about you?"

"Flute."

"Just flute?"

"A flute is like the Vietnamese language. Cheerful songs. There is no darkness in the flute."

"You're Vietnamese?"

"Half. I'm biracial. Vietnamese and Chilean." He laughed. "Biracial, trilingual and transgender."

"That's a lot."

"I'm everything at once," Sasha smiled. "That's what makes me so desirable."

Noah laughed. "Yeah, what more could I ask for?"

Sudden embarrassment seemed to overwhelm Sasha. "I'm sorry. Sometimes I just say what's on my mind. I was only kidding. I'm sorry."

"I know you were. But you are a pretty neat . . . guy. Is that right? I don't know. Am I supposed to say 'guy?' I don't know many. . . ."

"You are right any way you say it," Sasha said, a smile returning. "But I want to tell you my name. Call me Thanh. Sasha is for the others."

"Thank you," Noah said, but he was unsure he wanted to be in a special category.

"What do your close friends call you?" Thanh licked the foam off his upper lip.

"People call me 'Noah,' just 'Noah.'" Noah couldn't think of any close friends. "I don't care what people call me."

"You don't care what people think?"

"I've got to get a move on. Some things have come up." He nodded toward the phone. "You . . . um . . . need any money. I have a little."

"No," Thanh said. "I'm fine." He came over to Noah, stopped, rum-

20

maged in his bag for a card. Gave it to Noah. "My pager. Call me. I don't mean for a date like before. Maybe a movie, or something." He kissed Noah on the cheek.

"Thanks for the coffee."

Thanh nodded.

"Damn," Noah said shutting the door. He turned around, looked at his office. It felt empty. As if a huge vacuum had just sucked the life out of it.

His stale, uneventful, boring, going-nowhere life was getting complicated and very strange all of a sudden. He wasn't at all sure how he felt about it.

FOUR

THE DAYS WERE getting shorter. Noah hadn't noticed until now. It was dark when Noah boarded the ferry. Dark and cold. Winter, such as it was in San Francisco — mostly damp and gray — was approaching. The black sky was clear, a fact that became clearer to him as he reached the top deck of the old ferry and saw scattered stars twinkling. He couldn't remember the last time he saw starlight. Maybe he just hadn't looked in awhile.

Below, he could see a stream of passengers still boarding. Most of them in their career wear. The people who manage corporate images, mutual funds and various major lawsuits were deserting the Financial District, leaving hollow hallways to janitors and security guards.

Noah looked back at the skyline, still close, dramatic and ominous. He felt the wind, full of chill, rake across his face as he took a second look at the stars. The top deck was nearly empty. For all who boarded, few wanted to share the cold night with Noah, preferring alcohol and the warmth of huddled bodies on the crowded lower decks to get them through this short, but often choppy journey.

The idling engines revved finally. He knew they were on their way. He waited for her.

The ferry had already righted itself and cut at least a quarter of the distance to its destination and still no Olympia. He could see the twin-kling lights of Marin County well beyond the hulking mass of Alcatraz. The trip itself wouldn't last long, maybe only 20 minutes. Not much time. There would be time to talk if she'd show up soon.

He looked back at the city now. Distance was rendering it harmless and romantic — if that's not a contradiction, he thought. Bridges and more twinkling lights. He was caught between two twinkling fairy-lands. As he fastened the top button of his jacket, he caught the shape that neared him. Hooded. The grim reaper was his first thought.

"Why me?"

"What?"

"Why not Brinkman?"

"He looked like the kind of guy who'd sell out a client for the right price."

"And me? Saint or fool?"

"What do you want?" she asked with impatience.

"I need to know who you are," he said.

"I asked you to investigate my husband, not me."

"I don't need to know your life story. I just need to know for sure that you are Olympia Rawley."

"This is the address," she said. He felt a hand in his coat pocket. "Wait two hours, go there. It's near the dock."

"Won't I miss the ferry back?"

"It's not going back."

"Ever?" Noah asked, smiling, hoping he was only joking.

"Tonight," she said. "This is the last ferry . . . tonight." She turned her head, the shipboard light caught her smile.

She disappeared out of the small gathering of light. Gone. A mirage. Noah looked out at the Golden Gate Bridge. The fog waited on the other side, out in the Pacific, ready when granted permission to enter the bay. A matter of time. He reached in his pocket, held the small piece of paper under the light. Scrawled upon it was the name of a marina and a slip number. He'd be looking for a boat. It didn't say what kind.

That was it. He had his orders. Funny, he had this little tough speech prepared for her. But she was the tough one. Noah thought there was a time in his life that he was considered at least a little intimidating. Now, 12-year-olds in libraries and desperate women were pushing him around like a grocery cart.

Two hours. Enough time to have dinner. A good dinner. Why not? Some wine. He had the advance. He looked back across the ink-black waters of the bay to a more distant and even more magical San Francisco. It seemed almost foreign to him. He'd forgotten its charm, its power to

23

charge the imagination. He felt an invigorating chill on his face as the vessel bounced on the choppy waves. At least all this foolishness got him out into the world. If it weren't for the Rawleys, he'd be at some dingy bar killing brain cells. Now he'd do it with a little style.

By the time he'd descended the gangplank, most of the crowd had dispersed — in a hurry to find their cars for the remainder of their commute. He stood on the deck as it emptied, tried to get his bearings. Town first. Then the Marina.

Onion soup, steamy beneath the crusty cheese roof, and a glass of hearty red wine. Scallop risotto to come. Heaven, he thought. Noah could get used to this. He shouldn't, he thought. He didn't know how far the Rawley ticket would take him. But tonight, he was out. He was embracing life, such as it was, for the first time in a long time. Never mind it was in his own half-assed way. However this went, the gig was better than sitting in his car for ten hours on a stakeout.

The day had been modestly successful already. He broke down and bought James Morcham's attack book, *Collateral Damage*. And after some false starts in his attempt to find James Morcham himself — information had no record anywhere — he called the publisher, pretended to be the author and inquired what address their records showed. He hadn't received any correspondence for quite some time. He was mostly concerned with royalties, he told them. Noah — AKA Morcham — was transferred three times, finally getting a pleasant clerk probably parked in some accounting cubicle. She indicated they had received his letter requesting a change of address, and added in as friendly a tone as possible, "You're not due for another royalty statement until January."

"Please read the address you have for me anyway. I want to make sure it's correct."

She read it back. An address and a suite number in Calistoga. Morcham's book jacket said he "lived and wrote in the San Francisco Bay Area with his wife, Diane, and their two children."

Calistoga wasn't in the bay area, not even near it. He called information in Calistoga. Still nothing. But he had an address. It would take an hour and a half on a good day to get to Calistoga.

Was Morcham worth it? Maybe not, but Noah had nowhere else to go. The writer obviously considered Rawley an arch enemy. If Noah was

24

lucky, that passion might mean the writer was still keeping track of him.

Funny how you have to find a missing person to find a missing person. The entree came. The little scallops were crusty, singed on the outside, soft and rich on the inside. This wasn't Burger King. Another glass of wine. Noah hoped he didn't blur his mind too much. This conversation with Olympia was important. Given her propensity for secrecy, he might not get too many chances. He glanced at the second glass of wine. Shouldn't be a problem, he thought.

Because the fog came in as he dined, it took Noah a little longer than he'd thought to sort out the street-like grid of flimsy decks that made up this little water borne community. He could only see one or two vessels at a time and had to back track several times before he got the hang of the numbering system and found the right slip.

He was late. He kind of liked the idea of being late — a small, probably insignificant act of rebellion. One step aboard and Noah felt the surface give beneath his foot. He backed off a moment, then tried again, this time prepared for the floating world. Light seemed to be escaping from a window, the luminescence flattened by the fog. He looked around. He could be in Tunisia for all he knew.

"Hello!" he yelled. There was only one way to go, but he didn't see a way to get in. It opened before him.

"You made it," she said warmly. "Thank you."

Noah looked around. Her first. She wore jeans and a gray sweatshirt that hung loose over her lean body. Her hair, a dirty blond and not the hair she had on when she visited his office, was tied back in a ponytail. From what he could see of the boat, it wasn't at all what he expected. Certainly it wasn't anything he could afford, but it sure as hell fell short of the kind of craft the wife of a billionaire would own.

The nagging doubts he had about this whole affair suddenly seemed insurmountable.

"Mine, all mine," she said, smiling, as if reading his mind. "Charles doesn't know a thing about it. My modest little safe house. Wine?"

"Sure, I'm in Marin, aren't I? It's a requirement."

"I have scotch, bourbon, a pretty complete bar if you're more serious."

"No, I'm kidding," he said. "Bad joke. No joke, actually."

"Check my purse," she said. "There by the radio. Inside, you'll find a driver's license and a passport. I don't have my birth certificate, but that wouldn't give you the Rawley pedigree anyway. Also, over by the sofa?"

"Yeah."

"There's a picture of Charles and me in St. Kitts." She came back toward him, armed with large stemmed glasses, half filled with red wine. "I hope you like red. I come from the school that believes wine IS red."

The boat shifted and Noah nearly lost his balance.

"That's the good thing about living on a ship. You can always blame the bay instead of the alcohol," she continued.

"I might need that alibi later, if I can find my way back to land." He took a sip of wine. "Listen, I have to tell you before I take too much advantage of your hospitality, even if I buy you as Mrs. Rawley, there are a lot of holes in your story."

"Go on," she said, but she wasn't happy.

"Much like you, Mr. Rawley has his little escapes. He goes off for a month on one of his isolated retreats. Nobody, his bio says, goes with him. What makes you believe that he hasn't just popped off to some rain forest somewhere and decided you didn't need to know? Maybe he was pissed at you."

"He was going on his retreat — that day. The problem is he left his pack behind. He takes it with him every time whether he . . ." she looked at him sternly. . . "always takes it."

"Maybe he changed his plans and decided to camp out at some exotic spa instead?"

"His medicine was in the pack."

"What kind of medicine?"

"All sorts," she said, sitting on the sofa and patting it for him to do the same. He wondered if he should bark or just pant and wag his tail. He sat. "Most of it is for his heart. Necessary medicine. Vital. He wouldn't leave it."

"So you think his disappearance was a kidnapping timed to coincide with his usual trip?"

"I don't know. It could. This way they — whoever they are — have 30 days, or 27 now, I think — to do whatever they want with him before anyone even starts looking."

26

"Like what would they want to do? Wouldn't they want a ransom?"

"Maybe. Maybe they want information. Maybe they just want him dead or out of the way for awhile. I don't know."

"You could have called the police."

"I could have."

"But. . . ."

"Do you have any idea what news like that would do to the stocks of any number of companies around the world? Not to mention what it would do to my life." She had worked up a little anger. She paused, took a breath. "And what if you're right? Maybe he is taking his quest in a sauna somewhere?"

"All right, if I buy all of that, why on earth would you let all of that ride on some low rung P.I.? How can a little pipsqueak like me find a man like that? If he wants to disappear, he has all the resources in the world to stay hidden. If he was kidnapped, then it was by professionals, guys way out of my league."

"We've gone over this. It has to be kept quiet." Her eyes flashed. "I don't like to chew my cabbage twice, Mr. Lang. If you can't help me, you tell me right now. I don't have time to fuck around."

"Okay," he said.

"Okay what?"

"You'll get your money back. Most of it. I'll keep some for time spent and for you leading me on."

"I don't believe in leading people on," she said, now smiling. "I'm very direct. There are some legal papers, Mr. Lang. They have a major impact on how I'll spend my golden years. They take effect after he assumes control of a certain . . . international conglomerate. He assumes control in two weeks, even in his absence, unless of course, word gets out that he has been kidnapped or killed."

Noah still wasn't buying it. "I am waiting for the answer to the 'why me' question." She took a deep breath, then stared straight ahead. It was an angry silence. "I accept your motive," Noah said. "But not your solution."

She waited for him to continue.

"Charles Rawley could have been kidnapped by international terrorists and resides in a crate on a dock in New Guinea. Or he could be off on his isolated retreat in Tibet chewing on medicinal roots. You're intelligent. You can't possibly expect some down and out detective without resources to find him."

She shook her head. Another exhale. She shrugged.

"I expect to know more. If he was kidnapped for ransom, there will be a call. Every number of Charles' and mine has been forwarded to my cell phone. I keep it with me. I'm not in love with Charles, Noah. He's not in love with me. At least not in the conventional sense. But we have something. And with him gone, I'm scared. I'm alone."

"So you let your fingers run through the yellow pages?"

"I didn't pick you for your brain."

She took a sip of wine.

"Then is any of this important? It's just a pretense. If you just wanted a body, I'd have picked someone a little tougher than me. An ex-wrestler or something. You said the brain wasn't important."

"If you have one, all the better."

"What about his security detail? Surely, he has security. A man of his stature."

"They vacation when he goes off on this retreat. That's about the only time they can have any time to themselves. There's only two of them."

"Can we reach them?"

"I'd rather not."

"Why?"

"I don't trust them." She looked at her wine, an excuse to measure her words, perhaps deciding what to or what not to say. "I don't trust anybody."

"Except some randomly picked stranger?"

"A few thousand dollars later and he's finally catching on," she said.

Noah sipped wine and asked questions. She sipped wine and answered them. What he learned was that son, David, was nearly forty and had a wife and four kids. They lived in Greece, where he made very bad paintings.

"He thinks of his father's support as patronage in its noble, historic sense," Olympia said. "Actually he's being patronized. Charles likes the idea of David and his offspring on a remote Greek Island. . . ."

About Rawley's business interests, Olympia knew little more than what was in James Morcham's nasty book. Rawley had controlling or significant interest in major media corporations. The same went for one worldwide food producer, half a dozen energy corporations, and one or two weapon manufacturers. Though Olympia wouldn't verify Morcham's charges of Rawley's inspired and dangerous megalomania, she just smiled. She didn't smile when Noah explained that Charles Rawley seemed to own a dozen or so powerful senators as well— that his contributions, personal and through the maze of various and sometimes secret corporate holdings, financed entire campaigns. To say that chairmen of this or that committee wouldn't do his bidding was extremely naive.

Olympia suggested that all of this was probably a bit of an exaggeration. She let it go at that, now ready for this part of the evening to be over.

"You won't be able get back tonight," she said. "Too late." Her hand crept into the crevice between Noah's thigh and crotch. She pressed. The implication wasn't subtle. His response wasn't either.

"So you do have time to fuck around?" Noah asked.

"Now I do."

He knew how crazy it was. He tried to tell himself this wasn't a very smart idea even as he was led down narrow steps into a dimly lit cabin. He knew better. This wasn't wise. He knew better. He knew better. "This isn't smart," he said almost audibly. But he knew why he was doing this. It had nothing to do with the fact that she was attractive, that he had nothing better to do at the moment, and that he would no doubt enjoy it immensely. He knew the real reason. As he could have predicted he felt reassured when they undressed, when her palm closed around his rigid cock.

"Hi," he said to Olympia when she returned with two more glasses of wine. She climbed in bed, putting her drink on his belly. He used his free hand to steady it as she lit a cigarette. "Three a day," she said. "On special occasions, four. This was a special occasion." Her cigarette lit and in her mouth, she reached for the wine, but her palm stalled on the way, and gently caressed his languid sex until it stirred.

"Is this why you picked me?"

"Flattered?"

"I would be if the your other choice wasn't Brinkman."

"I had plenty of choices. Judging from your quick recovery, I made the right one." Content with the magic, she smiled and retrieved her glass.

He took a sip of his. It was very dry. Almost bitter.

"New bottle?"

"I've got a million of them. That's about what this one cost."

"I'm afraid you are wasting it on me. I have an uneducated palate."

"I know," she said. "You have a lot to learn."

FIVE

THE NEXT THING he remembered was a voice dragging him away from wherever he was.

"I'm sorry."

"Why?" he asked drowsily, looking around. It was the same softly lit darkness as before. "What time is it?"

"Time to go. I'm sorry I've got to throw you out."

"Mmmh?"

His eyes focused on her. She was dressed. Sweat shirt and jeans. "I don't want you seen here." She gathered his clothes and tossed them at him. There was no malice in her action. No warmth either. "It's a little after six. Still foggy. You can slip out and catch the first ferry back to the city."

"Yeah," he said. He couldn't come up with any argument to the contrary. Nevertheless he wasn't happy about the abruptness of it all. She went up narrow wooden steps and he could hear her clanking about above him as he dressed. She had a cup of hot coffee waiting for him, but that was about the extent of her hospitality.

"Do I warrant your cell phone number, in case I find or need something?"

"I'll call you," she said.

Noah was rarely up this time of morning. He grabbed another cup of coffee from a diner, taking it with him to the pier. He stood, huddled into himself, waiting for the ferry's gangplank to be extended. He wasn't sure he bought her story about needing him — just in case. But it made more sense than expecting him to actually find her husband.

Wavelets slapped against the hull of the ship. Seagulls screamed at the sunrise. In joy? In anger? Day was breaking. Was he ready for it? The smell of fish suggested death to him, and a fine coating of cold, morning mist dampened his face and his mood.

He looked in his wallet to make sure he had the money to pay for the trip. He hadn't taken that much with him, and dinner was more than he expected. But he was sure he had at least twenty dollars in his wallet. He was sure he had enough. He had more than enough. In the wallet, already stuffed with papers and phone numbers and God knew what else, was $2,000 in crisp, new $100 bills.

The money and the trip back changed his mood. The fog was retreating and now covered only the western half of the San Francisco skyline. The sky over Oakland was pink. Whatever could be said about what was going on in his life, at least something was going on. Life seemed bigger, more important, more interesting, more dangerous.

More dangerous. That thought lingered awhile. He was back out on the edge. That was good, wasn't it? He'd spent years in melancholy. Lately, he'd become completely disengaged. He couldn't even feel sadness. Now . . . introspection gave way to the outside world as the ferry neared its destination.

"Christ," he said, as the giant towers of commerce occupied more and more of the horizon, as his own smallness became more apparent. A tour bus was taking on passengers from the hotel on Market.

Someone in the torrent of worker bees swarming to the high-rise honeycombs mumbled "tourists" with disgust.

"Aren't we all?" Noah meant it, but the disgruntled, rushing pedestrian was too far away to hear.

His office never seemed more lifeless. As the long morning wore on, Noah thought that even an interruption by Sasha would be welcomed. He doubted that would happen. Noah was sure his visitor understood what was what by the time he left. He was sure the guy picked up on the unspoken message, much in the same way Noah picked up on Olympia's cool dismissal. "I'll call you," she said.

Only then did it occur to him that the money in his wallet was for services rendered. Was this an additional advance or had he been paid to give her pleasure? He'd been paid, just as he thought he was supposed to pay Sasha. The fact was that Sasha didn't take it. But he did. He had a hard time thinking of himself as a boytoy. He couldn't figure out if he should be insulted or flattered. He decided on the latter. "Just another pretty face," he said to himself and pondered the rest of the day. He decided to try the impossible — find the missing mogul — even though job performance expectations obviously didn't require it.

All she really wanted from him was to be "on call" in the event she needed him. "I'll call you." The more he thought about it the more amused he became. If she wanted to play little games, he could play a few himself. He picked up the phone, dialed information. "Pacific Bell, please." Feeling flush with all the new money under his seat and in his wallet, he was willing to pay the 50 cents to automatically connect him to Pacific Bell. He'd get her number, whether she wanted him to have it or not. When he got to customer service, he signed up for caller I.D.

Now what? He wondered when he'd completed that little act of defiance. Perhaps he should take the drive up to Calistoga, get what he could from Morcham. First though, he'd get what he could from the other writer, the one who co-authored the so-called autobiography. The blurb on *Quest* said that John Caldwell lived in Inverness. Information had two John Caldwell's there. One had to be the writer.

Noah hoped that he hadn't used up his appropriation of luck by finding the right John Caldwell on the first call. Surely he'd need it for more difficult tasks. But the correct Caldwell picked up midway through the message being left on his answering machine.

"This is John," the voice said.

"My name is Henry Marshall, Mr. Caldwell. I'm gathering some background information for a reporter for the *Journal*." Vague enough, Noah thought.

"What can I do for you?"

"We're doing a piece on the five most powerful people of America and one of those we're considering is Charles Rawley."

"I see."

"He's a hard man to talk to personally."

"Yes. Well they all are when they reach the rarefied air of the mountaintop."

"What was your experience working with Mr. Rawley?"

"You've read my book?"

"Yes, that's why I've been asked to talk to you. Get some quotes. If Rawley makes the top five, I'm sure we'll reference *Quest* in the story."

"You know how to provide a little incentive, don't you?" Caldwell laughed, no doubt picturing a fat royalty check. "Well . . . he was easy to work with. One of the best."

"He's not really known for being easy, Mr. Caldwell. That really was your experience?"

"Yes. I was surprised too, based on what I'd heard. Let me tell you something. I've written more than 30 biographies — all of them celebrities of one sort or another, all of them in collaboration. Only four of that 30 would allow my name anywhere in the book. Some of these idiots couldn't spell 'autobiography,' but they sure as hell wanted the readers to believe every little word came from them. That was never an issue with Mr. Rawley."

"Very generous, another trait not generally attributed to Rawley. At least not after reading Morcham's book."

Caldwell laughed. "Off the record. I can do that, can't I?"

"It will never appear in print, I promise," Noah said.

"Charles Rawley considered the act of writing something akin to basket weaving. He thought what he did was more important than learning a craft. He'd rather buy a basket than weave it himself. Writers to him were nothing more than scribes in the marketplace."

"Your book is very different than Morcham's."

"Yes, if you take five writers and put them in a room with a Granny Smith apple and ask them to describe it, aside from 'round' and 'green,' you will get no further consensus in the description."

"Aptly put. But these are pretty big differences."

"Yes, of course. I was asked to write Mr. Rawley's story as he saw it and do what we could to correct the public perception."

"PR."

"If you wish. As I suggested earlier, one's life is in the eye of the beholder. Mr. Rawley is a businessman engaged in free market enterprise.

Rawley and people like him are the new lords of the manors. They create jobs. They build economies. It's the real world — the way it really works, not the wishful and never existing utopia to which Morcham wishes to return."

"Rules of fair play?"

"As far as I know, Morcham has won or settled all alleged misdeeds in various and sundry jurisdictions. I know what you're after and I'm a little surprised you are taking this tack, being from the *Journal*."

"We ask a lot of questions. Our readers are aware of dark sides of some of these . . . uh . . . big people."

Oops, Noah thought. "Big people?" That was professional.

"Of course," Caldwell said. Unfortunately, Noah was sure he heard mistrust creeping into Caldwell's voice. "You said the *Wall Street Journal*. Let me do a little verification and I'll call you right back."

"No, I said 'Journal.' It's the *Missoula Journal* in Montana."

"Good God," the voice said, fading into a disconnection.

Noah put the phone down. That was a bust, he thought, deciding that he had to go to Calistoga after all.

"Big people," Noah said with disgust. "Noah Lang, you are one cool guy."

There was no direct route to Calistoga. Lots of small and smaller highways winding through vineyards. The fastest route was highway 38 to 29 and up through Napa Valley, through the little gourmet hamlet of Yountville, up through charming, bustling St. Helena where real estate offices outnumbered churches and finally into Calistoga, home of mud baths and spring water.

He stopped to gas up the car on his way out of the city. The automatic stop on the pump refused to work and splashed back. He was glad no one was smoking. He'd dry out. Across the street was an office supply place. He could pick up the caller I.D. device. Nothing but the best. Not only the number of the caller, but the name. He'd also get a cell phone when he got back to the city. It was absolutely necessary, wasn't it? Noah, inching his way into the information age, still remained decades behind the current investigative technology. He'd read about microphones the size of delicate earrings. He'd had demonstrated for him the mini video cameras that could record images in the dark. He knew about electronic homing devices the size of a stamp that could locate a snowball in a blizzard. Next life, he thought.

Once out of the bustle of traffic lights and off ramps, driving became a form of meditation. A little more than an hour after he crossed the Golden Gate, a relaxed Noah was pulling into Calistoga. He'd decided to enjoy the adventure. Take what comes. Enjoy it. So his client was treating him like a bimbo. So he slept with a transvestite or whatever Thanh was. It didn't matter. Noah would be alive until he died. That was the truth of it. The truth of all of it.

Calistoga was laid out like every town in old Westerns — Gunsmoke, High Noon. One long wide street with the front overhangs of stores and shops sheltering long, wooden, raised sidewalks. "Watch them swinging doors," he thought.

He pulled to the side and checked his crumpled map. The street he was looking for was right off the main drag. Right downtown, Noah thought. "This is easy." When he found the address, he realized it wasn't easy at all. Morcham's address was the local private mailing and packaging business. One rented boxes for the mail. The "suite" Morcham's address referred to was probably the size of a Wheaties box. Unless Noah was willing to stake out the place for a few days, the drive was a complete waste. He had the time, but not the inclination. Maybe there was another way.

"Hi," Noah said brightly to the young man behind the counter.

"What can I do for you," the fellow said, responding in kind.

"I want to get a mail box here in Calistoga."

"Good. What size were you interested in?" The clerk unfolded a small brochure that had the dimensions, their respective sizes and diagrams of the shape.

"Actually, the most important thing to me is the number. I need number 302."

"I'm sorry that's taken."

"You don't have to check anything?"

"No. He's a regular."

"You have a phone number on this guy? Maybe I could talk him into

36

switching."

"I couldn't do that."

"Really?"

"No, you could leave a note. I'd be happy to stick it in his box."

"Well, that's an interesting idea," Noah said.

"Then he could call you."

"But I'm not settled yet. I can't wait around for him to pick up his mail. Who knows when that would be?"

"Comes every morning."

"He does. Every morning?"

"One of the first customers. He comes into town for breakfast and checks his mail."

"Okay. Listen, let me think about this note thing. Maybe I'll check out St. Helena or maybe even the post office."

"We'd like to help."

"You've been helpful. I appreciate it." He'd find a little hotel or motel, have an early dinner. Go to bed.

Noah found a little motel on the way out of Calistoga on highway 128. Small, slightly tacky. It was amazing how much pleasure could be had from such a simple thing, a long, hot shower in this case. It was a shame to put on all the old clothes.

After dinner, a full and moderately mellow Noah retreated to his room, where he again skimmed Morcham's book. Skimming soon led to drifting and Noah awakened at the tinny sound of the clock radio. Again, he was up before dawn. If there was a downside to this job it was the seeming requirement to get up before the birds. The early bird gets the worm; but it sure as hell didn't pay the worm to get up early and, at the moment, Noah was beginning to wonder which role was his.

He wanted to be back in town, have a couple of cups of coffee to ignite his brain and be settled before Morcham made his rounds. He'd rather catch the guy at the breakfast table in some restaurant than on the street. But he'd settle for anything at the moment.

SIX

NOAH FOUND NO one resembling Morcham's dust jacket photograph. There weren't that many places to eat either. Perhaps he'd missed a side street. He'd have to stake out the store. At 7:30 Noah parked his car down the street from the postal business.

An elderly woman clutching a newspaper showed up a little before 8 a.m. and stood waiting. She was the first in when the young man opened the door. A few others, none of them resembling Morcham, came and went.

It was nearly nine, just about the time Noah was suffering two potential and usually conflicting catastrophes — caffeine withdrawal and a full bladder — when a man with silverish, curly hair entered the store. He walked hurriedly, worried about something. Maybe that was the way the guy was. Just generally nervous. The guy had a beard. Noah looked at the photograph again. Could be. The hair was right. The picture was at least two years old. A man could grow plenty of facial hair in two years. The glasses were different. Then he saw a flash of light as the sun caught shiny metal.

One of the man's hands was a hook, a shiny hook. Noah looked at the picture again. The black and white photo showed Morcham was standing in front of a doorway. In one hand, he held a book. The other was hanging casually to his side. He had two hands in the photograph. Noah retrieved his binoculars from the glove compartment. Little things, the size of opera glasses, wouldn't give him up close definition. But they would help.

Noah waited for the man to come out. Same nose. Same mouth. The silver hook was wired so that it could hold and pick up things. Noah

38

continued to examine the alleged Morcham. Had to be. The man didn't look at his mail. Instead he looked around as if expecting trouble, and walked hurriedly in the opposite direction from which he'd come. Noah started to get out, but reminded himself that he didn't want a confrontation on the street. As the man reached the corner, Noah pulled out slowly and made a turn. He passed the man, watched as he got into an old gray Volvo.

Noah decided to follow by being in front of him. It was a useful tactic when the prey was skittish.

They headed back out 128, toward the motel. Just past it, Noah saw the Volvo's left turn signal. Noah had a decision to make. The light changed. Noah decided not to take it.

Noah waited until the Volvo was out of sight before, moving off to the shoulder and, after waiting for a truck to pass, made a U-turn.

Whoever it was — and Noah believed the odds were 99 to 1 it was Morcham — it was a guy in hiding. A postal box instead of direct delivery. A beard. Maybe just a bitter, aging man who wanted nothing to do with the world. That was another possibility. But there was something furtive about the visit to the store. Maybe he was picking up some porn or something. Maybe . . . maybes didn't do the trick.

He was glad he didn't turn when the Volvo did. It would have been too obvious. The street was short and came to a dead end a hundred feet ahead. Beyond it were trees. Instead he went on, then turned and came back before making the turn.

Noah drove down the heavily wooded road, overgrown on the sides with ground cover and high, untended bushes. The street went half a block and stopped. No Volvo. There were two paths from the road — one to the left and one to the right — both wide enough for an automobile.

Noah drove back toward the main highway. He stopped, parked his car facing the highway. He walked back, down the isolated road, wondering which path to choose. What was it Yogi Berra was supposed to have said? "When you come to a fork in the road, take it."

This wasn't the path, Noah decided as he walked down the first break in the overgrowth. There were no tire tracks and low, weedy vegetation grew at random. At best, it was a walking route. Further in, he found a dilapidated cabin. The windows were gone and the roof had caved in. A few cans, cups and various wrappings dotted the area as did a few used condoms and beer bottles.

Noah walked back out into the little, dead ended side road. A desolate spot in the world. He walked with a little more caution down the second path. It hadn't rained, but there were some old, deep tire ruts in the earth. After a turn, the shiny aluminum of an Airstream trailer came into view. It was a small trailer, ten to twelve feet in length. Behind it he saw the front end of the Volvo.

His bladder reminded him of its condition. Noah walked back a few feet, out of sight from the road and from the trailer, and sent a blessed arc into some scrawny shrubs.

"What the hell do you want?" Noah heard the voice and felt something cool against the back of his neck. It felt like the barrel of a gun. It had to be Morcham.

"I'll put mine away if you put yours away." Noah stuffed his suddenly dysfunctional organ back in his pants and turned around slowly. Morcham's face was red with anger. Better red than white. Less dangerous, Noah thought as he tried to figure out how to handle this. He needed information, not confrontation.

Noah hadn't expected the shove. It caught him off balance and he bounced into the shrub before hitting the dirt. The gun was still on him. "I asked you a question."

"I'm no threat," Noah said, picking himself up off the ground.

"Get out of here."

"I need your help, Mr. Morcham"

"Who sent you?"

"I've read your book on Charles Rawley."

A nine millimeter pistol, Noah surmised. Maybe a Beretta. Not as bad as a .45, but at this range the point was moot.

"Who sent you?"

"I'm trying to gather some information for a story on. . . ."

"If I don't get a straight answer, you are a dead man. Who sent you?"

"I sent me, Mr. Morcham.

"Your name?"

"Noah Lang."

"How'd you find me?"

"I'm pretty good at tracking," Noah said, not wanting to get some innocent clerk at the publisher's office in trouble. "A little trickery. I'm no threat, Mr. Morcham. I want some information on Rawley, that's all."

"I don't have any."

"Surely you. . . ."

"All history. I wrote a book. The book is history. That's it."

"Listen. . . ."

"I'd rather let you go than shoot you."

"Well, now. See? We already have a lot in common and we've just met."

"I want to hear you say 'goodbye.'"

"Two minutes. Please."

"I'm serious. I'll shoot you and drag your ass halfway through a broken window. A break in. Clean and simple."

"All right," Noah said. "I'm sorry to disturb you." He walked down the path, then turned. Morcham was still there. So was the gun. It was a nasty thing to ask, but he had to ask it. "How'd you lose your hand?"

Morcham turned, walked to the trailer. He looked back — a hard stare. Noah took a few more steps to show he was leaving. He heard the door slam.

Could be that Morcham lost his hand in a hunting accident. A shotgun could do that. Now, he told himself, explain away the lovely wife and two children and the home in the Bay Area, the latter replaced by a very small trailer in Calistoga.

Okay, Noah thought, divorce. That explains the family and the loss of a home. A guy loses an appendage, loses his wife and children. Wouldn't all of that make anyone sullen and bitter?

However, the loss of the hand, the move to a tiny little trailer in the boondocks happened in the last two years - after the publication of a book — the nasty tidbits of which virtually sizzled on the page. Perhaps Morcham was a victim of vengeance and an example to those who would follow his lead. Noah's take was that the man lost his hand to primitive law. He'd used it to wrong someone. Noah already had guesses and was becoming obsessed with the possibilities.

Another thing. It was clear Morcham was hiding. Who from? The

41

same people who chopped off his hand? Made sense. It also made sense that Charles Rawley would rank pretty high on anybody's list of suspects.

By the time Noah got back to the city, the library was open. He spent the morning hours trying to find anything he could on the embittered writer. Noah found only one bit of information about him that appeared after the reviews of his Rawley book died down. In an interview published in one of the major papers, Morcham was quoted as saying that a new book about Rawley was in the works. And if they thought *Collateral Damage* was controversial, wait for the next one. A quick check of Amazon Books on the Internet showed no such book.

Back at the office, Noah set up his caller I.D. device and placed a call to the publisher — this time as a reporter for *The New York Times Book Review* — an inquiry of Morcham's editor got a friendly but terse reply.

"We've no word of that," she said.

That was it. If there were more to Morcham's story, and Noah knew there was, it remained out of the investigator's reach. Nothing he could do now, but suggest whoever was knocking on his door should "come on in."

Noah didn't like the looks of them. Two guys in ill-fitting suits. Were these goons sent by Rawley or Morcham or . . .

"Police," the first guy said. He flashed a badge.

"Whoa," Noah said, surprised.

"Are you Noah Lang?"

"That's an important question. Let me give it some thought."

"I'm Inspector Stern," said the big white guy. "This is Inspector Rose," Stern said introducing what appeared to be a blissfully disinterested small black guy.

"Homicide," Noah said. In San Francisco, the "inspector" rank was reserved for homicide detectives.

"That's right," said the guy who was apparently going to do all the talking. The other one, Rose, walked around the office looking.

"Who's dead?" Noah couldn't imagine. He didn't know very many people. Olympia? The last, but most likely possibility was Morcham. He'd just seen the guy. Someone may have witnessed the confrontation in the yard. That could be trouble.

"Gosh, Mr. Lang, I thought I was the cop." Stern acted confused, turned to his partner. "Am I the cop?"

"You're the cop," Rose said.

"I'm sorry," Noah said, amused.

"Then you'll let me ask the questions?" Stern continued as Rose opened the door to the bathroom. He went in. "Where were you last night?"

"Calistoga." No need to play games with the police. He'd learned that the hard way.

"That right?"

"Yes."

"You can prove that?"

"Am I going to need a lawyer?" Noah asked.

"I don't know, are you?"

"I've got a receipt from a motel just outside town."

"You mind if I take a look?"

Noah reached for his wallet, pulled out the receipt he'd kept instinctively for expense purposes. Inspector Rose crossed the room and went into the storage room.

"Hmmmmmn," Inspector Stern said. He handed it back.

"What is it? About an hour and a half from the city?"

"Yeah."

"Quicker at night when there's little traffic?"

"Maybe."

"Why were you in Calistoga?"

"A case I'm working on."

"What case is that?"

"I'm sworn to secrecy," Noah said.

"You hear that?" Stern asked his partner. "He's sworn to secrecy."

"Cool. I never get to do that," Rose said.

"You want me to swear you to secrecy?" Stern asked his partner.

"You know how to do it? Not just anybody can swear a guy to secrecy," Rose said, playing it all poker faced and low key.

"Maybe Mr. Lang here will tell us how that works."

"It's a client. I want to honor our agreement. Why don't you tell me who died."

43

"We might be sworn to secrecy," Stern said. "Are we sworn to secrecy?"

"Nobody has ever sworn me to secrecy," Rose said. "I told you. Maybe you've been sworn."

"Maybe I have," Stern said. "Okay, what about the night before. Where were you?"

"What night am I supposed to have done something?" Noah was getting angry. "Make up your mind."

"That's one of the nice things about being a policeman, Mr. Lang," Rose said. "We don't have to make up our mind. You do. What were you doing night before last?"

"I was with someone all night."

"And who. . . ." Stern started to ask. "Is that 'who' or 'whom', Rose?"

"Remember, we don't have to make up our mind."

"Okay. With who or whom did you spend the night?"

"I don't want to say."

"You don't want to say. Sworn to secrecy?"

"A married woman. It'd be a mess if. . . ." Now Noah was playing games. There were times when. . . .

"A woman?"

"C'mon, who died?"

"Remember who is supposed to ask the questions. That was earlier in the lesson."

"It's not my mom, is it?" Noah asked, hoping to shame them into a confession. His mother had been dead for years.

"Not your mother," Stern said. The inspector paused a moment. It worked. That little action, that little break in the cover, convinced Noah they were fishing. If they really believed Noah had killed someone, they wouldn't have worried about hurting his feelings. "I have a slip of paper here with the name 'Noah' on it, your address and suite number."

"And, we believe that piece of paper belonged to the victim." Rose finally seemed like a real cop.

Had to be her. Had to be Olympia. No one else had his number — well his phone number, that is.

"I got a couple of questions. You got a firearm?" Rose asked.

"No, don't believe in them."

"Good man. Any other kind of weapon?" Rose continued.

"Fingernail clippers in the drawer over there."

"Are they registered, Mr. Lang?" Rose asked.

"Do drugs?" Stern asked.

"Southern Comfort. Rolling Rock. Oh, a bottle of Nyquil."

"Ooooh," Rose said. "I liiiike Nyquil."

"You frequent prostitutes, Mr. Lang?" Stern interrupted.

"What?" It suddenly dawned on him. Rose's strange question about sleeping with a "woman."

"He asked you if you used the services of sex workers," Rose interjected from the corner of the office.

Noah's mind shut down. He didn't know what to say. They waited. No questions. "How did it happen?" Noah asked.

"I asked you a question. Have you ever paid for sex?"

"Christ!"

"You know who I mean, right?"

"Thanh."

"Sasha," Stern said, "as she is known to a good portion of the. . . ."

". . . transgender community," Rose interjected. "You have to learn these new words, Stern. Sex workers. Transgender."

"You availed yourself of her services?" Stern asked.

"We . . . uh . . . I didn't . . . I didn't know. . . ." Noah continued to struggle with incomplete syllables. Shame, shock and sadness seemed to be battling for dominance.

"Listen, Mr. P.I., I don't give a fuck how you get your rocks off. Girls, boys or something in between. A woman down the hall says she saw some young Asian girl leaving your office the other morning. I'm guessing you were the client, not Sasha."

"Okay," Noah said, defeated. "I . . . uh . . . what I mean to say. . . ."

"You could be doing it with horses for all I care, Mr. Lang. Let's get past this part. When did you see the victim last?"

"Two nights ago. No, day before yesterday in the morning. We had coffee."

"I see," Stern said. "And you mentioned you didn't know all about this little Sasha thing."

"She fool you?" Rose said, obviously done with his investigation of the premises.

Noah nodded. "Doesn't matter." The comment was meant for himself. This, out of the blue.

"What? You like drag queens?" Stern asked.

"No. Sexually, no. I like women."

"Really?" Stern asked. "And you say it didn't matter? You pick up a chick and the chick has a dick. That didn't bother you?"

"I thought you said you didn't care," Noah said.

"Oh, I don't, Lang. The question is how much you cared. How pissed were you when you found out she was a he?"

"How did he . . . how did the death come about?" All he could see was Thanh's face at the door. "Latte."

"Fire."

"An accident maybe?"

"No. Arson." Rose said. "For sure."

"Am I the only one on the list of suspects?"

"Don't you worry about other people. Just worry about yourself."

"We found some of the victim's clothing in the bathroom," Rose said. "Fire missed the bath. That's the only thing it missed."

"The little piece of paper with your name and number on it was in the pants pocket. That and a fake I.D. and a couple of twenties. That's the only stuff we found besides a body burned beyond recognition."

Noah felt tears rush up behind his eyes. What in the hell would he have to cry about? He met the guy. That was it. A few hours. A conversation. Why did he care so much?

"This is crazy. Stop playing the fucking games and tell me what's going on?" Noah shouted at Stern. He drew upon his anger to keep from crying, or whatever it was he was feeling.

"Maybe you ought to get a lawyer, Stern," Rose said. "I think he suspects you."

"I don't have an alibi either," Stern said.

"Look," Rose said with a little compassion. "What we want to know is what you know. That's all. You're on the list. That's for sure. But it's early. We're not taking you in. Let's not play tough. As Rodney said, we'll just all get along."

"You gonna cooperate?" Stern said.

"Yes." He calmed himself. He couldn't figure out why he was so emotional.

"Good. Let's start by you telling me about your secret client and your tryst with this mystery woman."

"You don't want my motel receipt from Calistoga?"

"If you want me to have it," Rose said, grinning. "It's small. It won't cost much to frame."

"It took two days for you to question me?"

"Stern had to attend his sensitivity class, didn't you Stern?"

"Yes. I now know you are an African American."

"Thank you," Rose said, then to Noah. "He's still working on the transgender community thing. Can you say 'transgender'?"

Noah didn't reply.

"Next week we find a new word for 'pervs,'" Stern said.

SEVEN

WHAT A STRANGE set of events. The reason why Olympia Rawley hired him was to make sure the investigation was a complete secret. Now he was being pressed by the very people she didn't want to know.

"Listen," Noah said. "I made up the client thing. I haven't had a real client in months."

"Why would you make up something like that?" Rose asked.

"I got drunk, spent the night with some prostitute."

"A woman?"

"Yeah. A woman."

"How about a lie detector test? We can clear up a couple of issues," Stern suggested.

"I don't believe in those things."

"Really?" Stern registered surprise with an exaggerated expression. "You're looking better and better for this thing."

"We're gonna need this other chick's name?"

"Look, it was a girl I met outside a bar over in the Mission."

"Yeah. Name?"

"Audrey."

"Now you're sure Audrey's a real chick?" Stern asked.

"Yes," Noah said, but at this point it didn't seem to matter. They already had their own ideas.

"Audrey? Audrey who?" Rose asked.

"I don't know." The only Audrey he could think of was "Hepburn." That wouldn't work.

"Where can we find her?"

"I don't know. We went to this . . . um . . . what do you call it? RV. We went to this RV, had some Tequila and uh . . . the next thing I know it was morning."

"Was she married or not?" Rose asked. "You told us she was married."

"That was the client story."

"Oh this is another story," Rose said. "I like stories. How many more you got?"

"I didn't want to tell you about the ratty life I lead."

Stern laughed, looked at Noah. "He kills me, Rose. The guy kills me. I half believe him."

"We're gonna need your prints," Rose said.

"You have those, don't you? I had to give them up when I got my license."

"State does," Stern said.

"We'll get 'em," Rose said.

Stern walked away, toward the door. "Take off your clothes."

"My clothes?"

"Hey Rose, was I accidentally speaking Chinese again?"

"Maybe Spanish. I couldn't tell."

Noah began to undress.

"Shorts too, doctor?" Noah asked.

"Yep, shorts, stockings, panties. . . ."

He went into the storage room, undressed as Rose stood in the doorway. A lot of people were pushing him around these days, Noah thought. He found some khaki pants and an old plaid shirt in a box. He hadn't worn them in years. Not exactly stylish, but he hadn't gone to the laundromat in two weeks.

"Where's your car?" Stern asked when Noah reemerged.

"Outside. A place in the alley. Why?"

"You got a trash bag or something?" Rose asked.

After Rose stuffed the clothing Noah had taken off as well as some of the dirty clothes in the hamper into a grocery bag, Noah walked with the two detectives to the elevator. Six floors down in a slow elevator. All was quiet. Noah was perspiring.

"Why do you want my clothes?"

"Rose's got a Halloween party tonight, don't you Rose?"

"That tonight? What are you wearing, dear?"

"A little silver number," Stern said. "Of course, I've gotta little trouble hiding my dick."

Inspectors Stern and Rose were especially interested in the metal gasoline container Noah kept in his trunk. It was a relic from 15 years ago, when he had a home and a lawn. But now it was clear why they wanted his clothes. The fire was started by gasoline.

"Anything you want to tell us?" Stern asked, more seriously now.

"No. I run out of gas sometimes."

"Used it all at the Trojan, uh?"

"The Trojan. Not the condom-inium. Thanh's building," Rose clarified before Noah could answer.

"Is that where all the gasoline went?" asked Stern.

"I have flares in there too. I haven't put on a fourth of July celebration," Noah said, getting angry again.

"Empty," Rose said, tapping the side of the little red gas tank.

"Yeah, well. . . ."

"Yeah well," Stern echoed, "you're in a heap of trouble." He took the can and closed the lid to the small trunk. "Listen, kiddo," Stern said, "stick around. Real close, huh?"

Noah nodded.

"Who you gonna screw around with tonight?" Stern asked.

"There's a gypsy caravan coming through here later," Noah said.

"Thatta boy," Stern said, not even close to laughing. "He kills me."

No word from Olympia the rest of the afternoon. Noah went to the gym, did a work out — a brief one. All he wanted was the shower. A long, hot shower. He called and checked his phone messages. None. It was still daylight. He could make it to Tiburon before the sunset and check out Olympia's boat. Doubtful she'd still be there, but it was worth a chance.

Olympia Rawley was his alibi — though she wasn't likely to admit it even if he could find her. But he had to try, while he was still able to walk around a free man. Sadly, to stay free he could use his ride on the gravy train. Maybe Olympia could say she hired Noah to do a background check on one of her employees or something. She could do that.

He hit commuter traffic. The wrong time for a trip to Marin. Then again, he might not have enough time to worry about such inconveniences. He'd seen the sunrise on the Bay. Now he'd see the sunset out over the Pacific. Big water. Big sky turning a lush salmon pink. Red sky at night, sailor's delight. He remembered that from his Navy days.

He wished he'd fixed the radio. Stalled on the bridge that suddenly turned into a parking lot, Noah was left with a mind to occupy. He'd done fine concentrating on the drive. Now he wasn't doing fine. One unpleasant image after another invaded. His mind was racing. The horror of Thanh's death was bad enough. But what about the horror of it being pinned on him? Add to that the inaccessibility of Olympia Rawley and the difficulty he'd have convincing her to cooperate even if he did find her.

He was convinced that he wasn't going to be tried for murder to protect Olympia's secret. It was a stupid idea to get involved in it anyway. The only good sign was that the police weren't likely to find his prints at the Trojan. And they weren't likely to find gasoline traces on his clothes.

"OH SHIT!" he said. He'd gassed his car on Geary, right before he stopped to buy the caller I.D. device. He'd been splattered with gasoline. His clothing might show that. He should have told them . . . like they'd believe him.

The guy was wearing aviator shaped sunglasses and a baseball cap. He was sanding down some trim on the boat.

"Hi!" Noah said.

"Hello," the guy said, looking at his visitor briefly and then turning back to his work.

"I'm looking for the owner of the boat."

"You found him."

"No, a woman."

"What you see is what you get, Mister."

"That's not how it's been going lately."

Noah looked at the boat. It looked like the boat. He checked the slip number. Right number. Fog clouded everything, including his mind, when he arrived that night and it was even worse when he left in the dark of early morning. Could he have been mistaken? He looked across the crowded neighborhood of tugs, trawlers, tugs and sailboats.

"Were you docked here last night before last?" Noah asked.

"I wasn't, she was."

"She?" Noah started feeling a little better.

"The Mascara. What you're looking at."

"Oh, the boat."

"The boat," the man said with disgust.

"You have someone staying over last night?"

"On board? No. What's going on here?"

"I was sure I spent the night here last night — with someone. I wanted to speak to her again."

The guy shook his head. "You one of those wackos Reagan let out of the loony bin in the eighties?"

"No. But I'm beginning to think that's where I belong."

"Could be."

"Would you let me take a look inside?"

"Tell you what," he said, standing up. "No."

"Please. . . ."

"I don't like anything about this conversation. If anybody was on board then, it was a break in. Now, why don't you take a hike."

It wasn't a question. But Noah did take a hike. Down the rickety patchwork of floating docks that led to hundreds of boats. Did he get the slip number wrong? Would he recognize the boat if he saw it? It was a dark and fog-filled night he'd wandered off to and away from. What he saw now looked entirely different in the soft pink light of sunset. What did he know?

Oh, he thought. He knew he was ineffectual. He knew he hadn't done anything right. He knew he'd lost control of . . . of everything. At least, he thought, I'm not without a clue.

Curiosity took Noah down into the Tenderloin where the Trojan apartment resided anonymously among other rundown apartment houses. Fire wasn't unusual in this neck of the urban woods. He didn't know which building was the Trojan, or even what street it was on; but the area wasn't huge, just notorious. Drugs and sex for sale. Whatever it takes to pay for a taco or a night off the streets. After ten minutes of bars,

Vietnamese restaurants, liquor stores, adult arcades and flophouses, he found the Trojan.

No sign of police presence. There was no evidence of fire from the outside. He found a place to park the car. On these days he was glad he didn't own a shiny new Lexus. No one takes pleasure in beating up something that's already beat up. Nothing inside to steal. He walked down the street toward the Trojan. The neighborhood was oddly quiet. It was early evening. Day people, taking care of day business, were gone. The night people hadn't emerged. He was surprised that the building was open for business. Apparently the damage was confined in some way. He went into the Trojan, a pale brick building with a dozen steps just beyond the bank of battered mailboxes, to get up to the first floor.

At the top was an older man in a wheel chair facing the entrance. A cane lay across his lap. Noah doubted the cane was used for walking. Beyond the gatekeeper was a half-lit hallway.

"What's your business?" he asked. The guy was old, unshaven, unkempt, inhospitable and obviously unhappy.

"Just visiting," Noah said.

"Who?" the man barked.

"Room number 307," Noah said, making it up.

"Who are you visiting?"

"The mayor."

"You don't have no reason to be here, take a hike."

"You have a relative . . . lives on a boat in Marin?" Was there no end to the number of people wanting to tell Noah to get lost? "You're not the first to give me those directions."

"You must be kind of an irritatin' fellow then."

Noah showed him his badge and tucked a $10 bill in the man's shirt pocket. "I'm harmless," he told the guy. "When was the fire?"

"Night before last," the guy said. "You an insurance man?"

"Nope," Noah said. "What floor?"

"Five," the guy said. "You can't go in there."

"I won't," Noah lied.

"Get yourself killed," the guy yelled at Noah as he went by.

The elevator was out of order. The stairway smelled of alcohol and urine. A young kid, tattoos forming a second skin on both arms, came hurdling down past him. At floor five, Noah emerged into an even darker hallway. Only two of the wall sconces had bulbs.

He checked the direction of the numbers and they didn't make sense, so he picked a direction. It was clear whatever rooms or apartments there were when the building was built, someone along the way saw fit to cut them up to get more rooms. Newer, badly cut openings had ill-fitting doors, some of them reinforced with raw plywood. Apartment numbers were rendered in black Magic Marker.

The direction he chose was the right one. He could smell burnt ash before he turned. This section was obviously in a separate wing. Maybe that's how they could keep the place open. These old flophouses were going up in flames on a regular basis, tossing hundreds out on the streets. With the shortage of low-income housing, that meant more and more homeless — already an epidemic. Where the hallway ended, he saw black walls, black doorways. A yellow police ribbon crossed the hallway. Three of the apartments on the fifth floor were charred by the fire.

Noah slipped under the ribbon and looked in the rooms, from the hallway. Some of the floor was gone and even where he stood, he felt a little give. Noah backed away, looking for solid ground. He wasn't about to go into any of the rooms. He wondered which room was Thanh's. Did it matter?

He wondered why it mattered to the police. Guys on the edge like Thanh weren't usually a high priority unless they made the news. As far as Noah knew, Thanh was just a victim, unless his room was where the fire started.

"The night of the fire," Noah said to the old man, "did you see strangers come through here?"

The old man looked at him with contempt.

"You were here, right?"

"Strangers?" the old man asked. "They're all strangers."

"This your place?"

"No. I just look out after the owner."

"You'd remember if someone came in with a large container, something that could carry gasoline, wouldn't you?"

"I talked to the cops," the man said, fumbling for a cigarette.

"I'm trying to help somebody who died in the fire."

"Didn't know 'em."

"I didn't tell you who it was."

"Don't know nobody," the man said.

"You didn't see anything suspicious."

"Everything's suspicious. You think I don't know what goes on around here? People comin' and goin' at all hours. You don't think I know what kind of things happen here?"

"I'm sure you know. I figure you know a whole lot."

"I know what you're gettin' at. But I can't help you partner."

"You know a Sasha or a Thanh?"

"The one the police say burned up there."

"You don't know him? Asian, Hispanic."

"Not in particular. Lots of coming and goin'."

"You collect the rent? He would've paid rent. People don't live here for free, do they?"

"It's all cash. Don't remember one Oriental from another. Bunch of Vietnamese around these days. Don't know where they all came from all of a sudden. The war was over years ago."

The kid who came tumbling down the stairway was coming in the front door with an older man. The new friend wasn't exactly wearing Armani, but he was a little too well-dressed for the neighborhood.

"Catch you later, Sid," the kid said, tucking some bills into the old man's shirt pocket. The reluctant companion looked a little frightened. His eyes checked every inch of this wretched place and didn't seem at all happy about it.

"Collectin' the rent, eh Sid?" Everybody's got an angle to work, Noah thought as he descended the steps out into the street. Looking out for the owner. He wondered how much of Sid's commission the owner saw.

Noah needed a drink.

A couple of steps toward his car he decided he needed food. He wasn't hungry, but he'd had nothing all day. Even a couple of beers on an empty stomach would cloud his already cloudy mind. He knew of a Thai restaurant in the neighborhood that was cheap and good.

Bad idea. The young waiter reminded him of Thanh. Slender, friendly, graceful, gentle. What was Noah doing, anyway? Thanh, no matter how rotten a deal he got, was in the past. He was history. What wasn't history was the trouble his death had made for Noah. Noah took a healthy swig of beer to punctuate his thought. He couldn't dwell on Thanh's death. Hell, he hardly knew him.

The waiter delivered the second bottle of beer. A polite smile. Again, Noah noticed the similarity. More boyish, but pretty. . . .

"God," Noah said out loud. He shook his head. Slender. Graceful. What in the hell was he thinking? He had to be careful not to let his mind out — except on a leash. His thoughts were foreign to him. And what in the hell was he doing out here anyway? He couldn't bring Thanh's killer to justice, for Christ's sake.

Right now he needed to keep his mind on Olympia. He thought of her on the boat. It was good. He enjoyed the uninhibited sex. He didn't like her. She was cold, mechanical, but it was good. He liked Thanh better — as a human being. Oh shit, he thought. As a human being, he reminded himself. His mind had a mind of its own. Forget about it. Why did he care? He didn't. Not about either one of them.

One of his clients once accused Noah of having a Zen mind, because he didn't judge. Didn't keep thinking about monkey mind issues like right and wrong and good and evil. A Zen mind. Noah couldn't figure out the difference between Zen and indifference. But now his judging mind was busy trying to sort out all sorts of things. One thing at a time, he told himself. He needed to find Olympia. If he didn't find her, nothing else mattered anyway.

He'd give her until tomorrow. If she didn't call, he'd go out to the house. He'd break the rules. Had to. He thought he'd settled it. Thought he'd put a plan together for tomorrow and the night would take care of itself. But it didn't.

On his way back to his Alfa Romeo, Noah stopped at a place called "Dan's" something or other. Added a Rolling Rock to the two Thai beers he had with the Satay chicken.

Right now, just think about finding Olympia, he kept telling himself. She was the alibi. She could also answer questions about the guy on the boat.

Basketball was on television, a Pacer-Warrior match that no one watched. The seedy environment was enlivened with Christmas lights strung, along with gold garlands, on the wall. Cheap sentiment. People die all the time, don't they? It's a goddamn nasty world out there sometimes. He noticed the dust on the little colored bulbs. Christmas all year here in Dan's. Yeah, let's make sure we don't spoil the depressing atmosphere. He thought about going over to the jukebox and playing some country and western tune and maybe shooting himself.

What did he know about the guy, anyway? Sasha, Thanh, whoever in the hell he was. Another lost soul. There were a lot of them, especially here in the Tenderloin. Living on the edge. Clinging to life by their fingernails. Damaged goods. Sexually confused. Slipping way out of the mainstream. They weren't likely to be friends, he and Thanh. What did they have in common?

He left Dan's something or other and went out into the dampening night. But he knew he wasn't going home.

The place was close by. Another Tenderloin bar. He could walk it.

EIGHT

Noah had been in a lot of bars in his three plus decades of existence. On the surface, this one wasn't in any way exceptional or even unusual. Could have been a little bar in a motel just off a highway in Omaha. One wouldn't pick up on the special ambiance in the first few seconds. For some, it would take minutes.

Though Noah had never been inside, he knew it wasn't your average Holiday Inn kind of lounge, despite the fact that the guys sitting at the bar and at the little tables lining the mirrored wall, looked as if they were traveling salesmen or accountants attending a convention.

The place was nicer than Dan's Something or Other. Clean, with mood lighting. With the clink of glasses, the roll of dice in a leather cup, slapping on the Formica, it could have been a sports bar near a baseball stadium. No one would know right away. Over the sound of conversation and jukebox music were the yelps of the winners and good natured bickering. Then it would sink in. All the girls were dressed to the nines. Mostly in black, with exaggerated makeup and theatrical mannerisms.

Noah went to the bar, squeezing between a pungently scented being and an electronic poker machine. On the back bar, next to the cash register, was a split screen television monitor. One viewed the street just outside the front door. The other must have been the alley. He got a Rolling Rock from a young Asian man, whose plaid shirt and jeans suggested he was content with tradition. Noah left him a dollar tip and sat at one of the little tables along the side.

"You mind if I sit with you?" The person requesting the seat was all bosom and butt. He'd seen her when he came in. What had been done to her waist was magic. It barely existed. Breasts and buns were another

58

matter entirely. She was quite a girl. And, apparently she wasn't the kind of girl to wait for an invitation.

"Where you from?" she asked, voice husky, sipping her drink through two skinny straws.

"Here," Noah said.

"You born right here at this table? My, that's something. How does it feel to be home again?"

"I'm looking for someone."

"Aren't we all, honey."

"Sasha."

The big toothy smile and the dancing eyes vanished. Her face became the fifth on Mount Rushmore. She got up, went to the bar. She and the bartender talked. The bartender shook his head.

"You might have set a record," said a tall blond in a short black dress.

"What?"

"She can usually go a few rounds after the brush off," the blond smiled.

"I think I said something wrong," Noah said.

The blond sat. All legs. Nice legs.

"I'da thought she heard everything by now. Why don't you try me? If I haven't done it, I probably haven't heard of it." A smile. A charming smile.

Her shiny short skirt riding up to her thighs.

"Sasha. Looking for friends of . . . hers."

"Ooooooh, I see. . . ."

"Don't be telling tales outta school, Miss Thing," said Miss Bosom and Butt as she passed by.

"Let's go back to 'oooh, I see.' What do you see?" Noah asked the blonde.

"A cop?"

"Private."

"Not too private, I hope," she said, putting her hand on his. He noticed her hands were every bit as big as his, but the nails were more expensive.

"You know her?" Noah asked, gently pulling his hand away.

"Show me something official. Don't you guys have to have a license or something."

Noah complied.

"Well, Noah," she said. "Who do you work for?"

"Me."

"You."

"I knew him."

"Really?" The way it was said said it all, "And I know Julius Caesar."

"I'm impressed. I often eat his salad. Thanh and I talked a little bit. The cops talked to me. For some reason, I feel compelled to look into his death."

"Who said his name was Thanh?"

"He did. Isn't that his name?"

"Yes, it is. He doesn't tell everybody. You know my name?"

"No."

"Good. Keep it that way. You mind?" she said, pulling a cigarette from her little black bag. She inhaled, let a 1940's cinema cloud of smoke roll out between her ruby red lips. Pretty white teeth. Noah thought about rewriting the Goldilocks tale, one in which the wolf is the victim.

"I'm looking for leads."

"Not company for the evening?" The blond smiled again. Big smile. She was playing.

"No. Not tonight."

"Hubbard."

"What?"

"Hubbard killed her."

"Who is Hubbard?"

"Boyfriend, husband . . . whatever."

"Why?"

"Sasha left him."

"Why?"

"Maybe she wanted to reach thirty. Maybe she just wanted to stay pretty."

"You didn't tell the police this?"

"Didn't talk to the police. Don't talk to nobody. Haven't been talking to you."

She stood.

Noah wanted more information.

"During this conversation we never had, did I ever figure out Hubbard's first name and maybe his address?"

"Don't know his full name name. Goes by 'Zip' as in 'nada,' as in 'zero,' cause that's what he gives you. Has a condo up in Specific Heights."

"Speaking of 'specific,' could you be a little more?"

"I never had the displeasure. He likes minorities only. Asians, blacks, Hispanics sometimes. I think he pretends to be a slave owner. Don't cotton to blondes, though. Thank God."

"Does he come in here?"

"Funny you should ask. He was in last night. Early. Before ten. Lookin' for a new bride, I think."

"Did he find one?"

"I don't think so."

"Thanks."

"You like blondes or are you just into Asians too?"

"Blondes are nice," Noah said.

"Nice?" The blonde laughed. "Is that what you're looking for?" She shook her head in mock frustration. "Then again," she said. "Let me go change into my Gidget outfit."

"Thanks again."

"Your loss," the blond shrugged. "Anyways, puttin' you onto Zip wasn't doing you any favors."

The blonde left. Noah left half a glass of beer and headed for the door. Enough for tonight Noah thought, noticing the little stage for the first time — empty except for a gold-gilded French Provincial fainting couch.

Standing near the stage was another blonde, this one quite perky. She wore her hair in a long ponytail and was prancing about in a cheerleader's outfit. Short skirt, tall white boots. She'd lifted her skirt revealing every inch of her pretty, pin-up quality, barely-thonged pale butt.

Noah went outside thinking that God had made at least one serious mistake. If he, or she, really wanted to make the sexes different, they wouldn't have been given so many similar parts.

Well, there it was. Plan B. He'd almost dismissed it. If he couldn't entirely depend upon Olympia — and he couldn't — then maybe he

61

could find the demon who set the fire. This Zip guy looked pretty good for it, apparently, and Noah had nothing else to do until Olympia called or until the police locked him up.

But, it was too late, and he was too tired and confused to try to make the day last any longer than it had. Hubbard, whoever in the hell he was, could wait. At home, Noah stripped down to his shorts, grabbed the blanket and pillow from the basket in the corner and stretched out on the couch. He got up, flicked on the TV, and searched for a clean sheet to put between the cold vinyl and his flesh.

Christ, he'd have to do laundry one of these days — oh yeah, his dirty clothes were gone. Tomorrow, let's see, he thought. Then out loud, "Find killer, stay out of prison." Simple enough. On TV, David Letterman was dancing with a dog. The world was no doubt unfolding as it should.

Noah hated waking up to the sound of someone knocking on his door. It was only eight. Who were these Neanderthals? Could be Olympia, he thought. God, could be the cops.

"Who is it?"

"Brinkman."

Noah opened the door in his skivvies. Brinkman held in his hand a box.

"Aren't I supposed to be wary of Geeks bearing gifts?"

"Something like that," Brinkman said, squeezing into the office, un-invited. He looked around, glanced toward the bathroom. "Least you could do is wear a tie." Brinkman looked back to Noah.

"You looking for something. Lose a dog or just nosy?"

"Take your pick," Brinkman said. "There is something untoward happening here. Of that I am quite certain."

"Has your jib healed?"

"Quite nicely, my lord."

"I keep forgetting to ask. You were a thespian in some previous life?"

"You said thespian?"

"Yes."

"Of course," Brinkman said. "I had quite a flair. I had the lead in that great play, 'Testiclees and Clitoris.'"

"And what part did you play?"

62

"You are a jealous man," Brinkman said.

"No. Me? I was in a drama recently. 'Androgynees and' . . . never mind. What is this?" Noah asked, placing the box on the desk and going for his pants.

"I have no idea. It was addressed to you, but not finding you at home, it was delivered to me. Being an honest and. . . ."

"The way my luck is going, it's probably a bomb."

"I noticed the boys from homicide were here."

"Yes."

"Questions about the little pecan tart you've been frequenting?"

Noah felt the anger rise. He was able to squelch it before it turned verbal; but Brinkman got the idea and changed the subject.

"Aren't you going to open it?" Brinkman asked. That was why he was hanging around. It was great, Noah thought, that one could make one's natural nosiness a business.

"The package? It'll wait."

Brinkman was clearly disappointed. "I checked down at the station."

"About what?"

"About you."

"What did you find out?"

"Traces of gasoline on your clothes."

"And that means?"

"Yeah, what does that mean?"

"You got more than that," Noah said.

"You're pretty high up on the list. Actually you're the only one on the list. Want some help?"

"I appreciate it. Maybe later."

"Professional discount," Brinkman said, slipping out of the door.

Noah opened the box. In it was a small, cellular telephone. The note read. "Things will happen soon. I may have to reach you immediately. Keep this with you at all times." The words "all times" were underlined.

It wasn't signed. Let's see. Which client could this be? Maybe the only one he had. "Dammit, Olympia, you could have called." He couldn't ask her about the boat, about an alibi, about spending another night together. If she had called him on his phone his new caller I.D. feature would have recorded her phone number.

Noah checked out the phone. Dialed information. Asked for an address of a Hubbard in Pacific Heights. When pressed for a first name, he said "Zip." He got zip. He gathered his dirty clothes, towels and sheets, grabbed his new phone and left.

Laundry. Workout and shower. Lunch. That was the plan.

If he received no call from Olympia, maybe he'd take a little ride over to Tiburon. Look at boats. The foggy night he spent on board the "Mascara" — or its twin — bothered him. So did Morcham's hook, not to mention his demeanor. And there was a guy named Hubbard to add to the list.

Clam chowder at a little place he knew down from Russian Hill slowed his metabolism down to a manageable level. Now he was back on the Bridge. It was becoming a familiar route.

Catching her on board would be a long shot. Second best would be to be able to take a look inside and see if someone — Olympia or the old coot from yesterday — was giving him the runaround.

The option of tracking her down at the mansion in Hillsborough was still viable — but that would shut down the relationship and the flow of money. That was the choice he'd make shortly before the sound of prison locks fell into place.

Sunny, warm. Another day in paradise. There was always a question about whether San Francisco was in California, or whether the giant state merely surrounded a strange and sovereign entity. There was no mistake about Tiburon, however. Like its sister, Sausalito, it was definitely California. Tofu, sunlight, convertibles and blondes real and imagined.

A surprisingly buzzing marina reminded Noah it was Saturday. But he would not confront Olympia or the old coot. He would not be able to take a look inside. The "Mascara" was gone.

A sailboat occupied the slip.

"Hello!" Noah yelled.

A teenager in Nautica shorts and tennis shoes came from the stern.

"You here about the boat?"

"What about the boat?" The world was beginning to get a little too surreal for Noah's down-to-earth soul.

"For sale," the kid said.

"No, actually, I was here to see the boat that was in this slip yesterday."

"This is our slip," the kid said. "At least until we sell this."

"You weren't here yesterday."

"Came in this morning. Needed some work. It's seaworthy now."

"Yeah." Noah said. "You know anything about a boat called the 'Mascara?'"

"No."

"Thanks."

"Tell your friends," the kid said, his hands waving back over his vessel, "about this dream."

About the dream? For a moment, Noah was puzzled. Until he realized that 'dream' meant the boat and not some vague reference to Noah's state of surreal consciousness.

NINE

NOAH WAS MORE successful getting his laundry than he was in finding the Mascara. The dock master had no record of it. The slip belonged to Thomas V. Moore. Moore owned a sailboat called "Chipper's Block." Giving in to the great unknown, Noah settled for a workout and a Big Fish Value Meal at Burger King.

The meal sat a little heavy — and he hadn't had anything green, let alone leafy, in several weeks — but he felt good. A hot shower. Clean clothes. If he wasn't looking forward to an evening surrounded by transvestites and the men who loved them, he looked forward to the beer. Little pleasures meant a lot.

Noah was at the bar by eight-thirty, listening to Rap or Hip Hop or something. The bartendress and a customer were heavily engaged in the shaker slamming, obsessed with the tale of the dice and keeping track of accumulative dots on a piece of paper. Three others were at the bar. A young guy in a black shirt that said "security," an old, but apparently game, drag queen sipping a bluish illuminated iced drink through lipstick tipped straws, and a stylish Asian girl or boy in black. Bigger boned than Sasha, but attractive. He hoped he wasn't enjoying this too much.

The blonde from the previous night was sitting at a side table with an older man in glasses. The man was a classical sort. Maybe he played the cello in a symphony. Could be a doctor. Maybe a psychiatrist. Probably a psychiatrist who played the cello.

Noah hoped it wouldn't be a long night, though in fact, he was beginning to like this bar better than his usual hangout. People were engaged in life here, not dog-paddling in place until it ended. He ordered a Rolling Rock. That and a not necessarily generous tip took care of a five. Music changed. Madonna, Noah guessed. What the hell did he know? He just knew it wasn't Janis Joplin or Peggy Lee.

Television was on. Sports. Mute. Seemed out of place. But what did he know? Noah took his little green bottle to a side table, picking a seat with a view of the monitor that showed who was coming in the front door in gritty black and white. A couple of guys, looking like high school seniors, came in, paid no attention to the clientele, and went back through a door in the back. Not the johns. Another, unmarked door. Noah wondered what went on back there, thought maybe it was better not to know.

Noah saw a figure coming in. Jogging suit. Expensive jogging suit. Noah would have cast him as a stockbroker from Mill Valley. He didn't have to tell the bartendress what he wanted. An attractive Asian at the bar smiled a hello. This new customer kissed her on the cheek and went over to the juke box. The guy didn't look gay. Who did? Half the bar's patrons didn't look gay, whatever that meant anymore. The other half looked like women. Some of them were, he surmised. Some weren't.

Within the next hour and during three of Noah's Rolling Rocks, a number of guys and girls showed up. Real girls, some of them, Noah was sure, but unwilling to stake his life on it, however. Nerds, down and outers, truck drivers. The truth was no other bar he knew of cut a wider swath through social strata.

The place was getting busy and Noah wondered if any of them was Zip Hubbard.

"Excuse me sweetheart," he could hear the blonde tell her cello-playing friend. "I'll be right back." The blonde walked down to the jukebox and looked for a moment, then returned, eyeing Noah. "The guy in the Italian knit and the leather jacket," she said in a whisper and kept walking.

He'd watched earlier as the guy tried to speak to two attractive Asian "girls." The two were nervous. One of them giggled. The other shook her head "no" and pointed to her watch and both girls left the bar. Now the guy in the Italian shirt was sipping his drink, quietly, eyes occasionally scanning the bar, always checking the newest arrival.

Zip Hubbard was dressed well. The shirt had to have cost him a few hundred and the leather jacket several hundred more. Noah didn't know what the label would say, but this jacket looked too good to be off the rack at Macy's. The guy wasn't bad looking either. He was about the same size as Noah, same hair even; but had broader shoulders and a flatter belly. Fit. In shape. Zip was older than Noah, but probably in the same generation.

None of this was what Noah imagined a guy named "Zip" would look like. He'd somehow pictured some furtive, slobbering creep in brown polyester. This wasn't the case at all. Maybe he'd go up to the guy, strike up a conversation. Then he thought that probably wasn't a good idea. He didn't want things to get out of hand in a public place. Also, it was a good idea to know a little more about Zip. What he drove, where he lived, where he worked. Noah, despite the fact that he could be arrested at any minute, would wait and follow. It was time to start doing something right.

His third beer was gone. He could handle four and still think straight. He'd get one more and make it last for as long as it took. He hoped that didn't mean he'd be there until closing.

The blonde left with the cello player. The Mill Valley jogger left alone. Others came and went, some of the girls several times. He was pretty sure some of them had regular spots on the streets, spots they'd leave when police activity increased. The bar was still half full. Noah told himself a number of imaginary stories about the clientele and, by midnight, had still managed to maintain half of his fourth bottle. He was proud of his self control.

He kept his glances in the direction of Zip Hubbard at a minimum. Not only did Noah see no reason to spook the guy, but each time he looked at Zip he remembered Thanh and the fire. He didn't like the images floating through his brain.

But he was still puzzled by Zip. This guy looked too together to be that vengeful, that insane. With his looks, apparent money and the plethora of desperate immigrants looking for financial support, it wouldn't take a guy like Zip very long to replace a lost love, would it?

Zip left. The movement was clear. A glance at the watch, the downing of his drink and he was on his way. Noah checked the monitor. Zip

68

turned right. Noah left half his beer, went out. A Porche Boxster. Silver. Noah got out in time to see him duck down and into the sleek sports car.

Noah walked the other way to retrieve his rusty, raggedy automobile. He might have been too late. He should've come outside and waited in his car. Private Eye 101. Oh well, hell. The car was gone. Noah was sure there was no way to find him. If Zip lived in Pacific Heights there were a dozen ways to get there. And a car like that would end up in a garage not on the streets.

He cruised the neighborhood just in case. And if no luck had come his way so far, it appeared to be doing so at the moment. A silver Porche Boxster was on Eddy near Larkin. A tall, slender black woman was leaning down, chatting through the passenger window. Noah thought it was one of those who had paraded in and out of the bar.

Noah stopped, pulled into a "no parking" zone and waited. After a few moments, the figure got in, closed the door. The Porche brake lights flashed for a second. Zip was leaving and apparently taking his "date" with him. Noah followed around the block and up Polk Street until the car turned into Hemlock Alley. Turning there would be a giveaway. He went by the alley and double-parked, put on his flashers. He got out and glanced down the alley.

The Porche was parked midway down the alley. Lights off. Noah couldn't see much — the shadowy shapes of two heads in the back window. In a few moments, one head disappeared. This could take a while. But Noah had to be ready. When Zip was done being done or whatever, he would be forced to turn left out of the alley onto Larkin because the alley came to a dead end at Larkin. And he had to turn left because Larkin was one-way north. Zip had no choice. That made it easy for Noah. All he had to do was park on Larkin and pick up Zip after he made the turn.

Even so, Noah almost lost him. The Porche was pulling out just as Noah made his turn on Larkin. Either that was the quickest of the quickies or this was sex to go. Noah followed the Porche at a discreet distance, picturing him disappearing into a massive garage beneath a high-rise apartment building. What if Hubbard didn't use his name on the mailbox? How could he visit the guy?

Zip made it easy. He lived in a house not a high rise. Modest by Pacific Heights standards, the small Victorian would sell for a high seven figures just because of the neighborhood. Across the street was a huge park on the rise of the hill — Alta Plaza. The door to Zip's sunken garage opened automatically and the Boxster pulled down the slanted drive into the hole.

Noah wanted to wait, but a car of the Alfa Romeo's dilapidated presence, would be noticed, especially hanging out there in the middle of the street. He moved on slowly, but saw the two of them emerge from the garage.

"Hmmmn, take out," Noah said. The tall black woman with a leopard skin bag, long legs and spike heels was being hurried into the front door.

Somehow Noah couldn't imagine her spending the night and having scrambled eggs and orange juice in the breakfast nook the next morning. Then he reminded himself. He knew nothing at all about these things. Should he wait? Would he drive her back to the Tenderloin? Would he call a taxi for her? Perhaps Noah could pay him a visit in the wee hours of the morning. Let the bastard slip off into dreamland and while Zip the pyro was at his most vulnerable, become the creep's worst nightmare — squeeze out some information.

This, of course, would have been a better idea if Zip Hubbard was the roly-poly loser Noah had imagined him to be. But it would still work. The average guy, especially if he's surprised, wilts under surprise aggression. Then again, Noah thought, this guy was a murderer. Yeah, but what kind of murderer? Someone who can't face his victim. Sneaky. Cowardly. The lowest of the low could do that.

Noah would wait. He drove around the park several times, finally finding an illegal, but less obvious spot on its perimeter. Perched on a bench on one of the park's high green terraces, he watched the house. Whether Zip was Thanh's lover, partner, or sugar daddy, the younger Thanh had lost a good gig — looking at it materially, that is — before losing his life.

Hours later, the increasingly restless watcher stood for the dozenth time to stretch his legs. He pressed the little button on his watch. His eyes had trouble focusing on the numbers. Best he could make out was that the big hand was on eleven and the little one was right on four. The night chill had kept him awake, but he wasn't sure how much longer it would be a factor. He had just about decided to finish up with Mr. Hubbard at a later date, when he saw the familiar colors of a Luxor Cab pull up in front of the house. A tall slender black human form, looking more male without the wig, ran out to the cab.

The light from the open doorway became narrower and narrower until it disappeared. And the cab accelerated down the quiet streets. Noah would count to sixty. Then he'd pay Mr. Hubbard a visit, despite the twinge in his stomach. His body knew, if his mind didn't, that despite his patient waiting, Noah was acting impetuously, foolishly.

He knocked. The porch light came on, a politeness Zip hadn't provided his date.

"I'd like to talk to you," he said to the man who answered the door wearing the kind of plush terry cloth robe you get in very nice hotels.

Hubbard opened the door.

"Nice butt," Hubbard said as Noah stepped inside.

"What?"

"Jolie. You're the irate lover or something, right? Anyway she was very good at what she does." Hubbard turned, walked away, then turned back. "No," Hubbard said sharply, then smiled. "You were at the bar."

"No, I'm from the neighborhood association. We've had complaints that you have a nasty way of ridding yourself of ex-lovers. Setting them on fire is a violation of the Pacific Heights Good Neighbor Honor Guide."

"I've got a thing for faces," he said, walking back into the living room, grabbing his drink from the table. "You sat at a little table by the wall."

Noah didn't know whether the room would be considered in good taste or not, but he was sure it was expensive. Soft black leather on both sofas and all four chairs. Lots of metal and glass. Masculine, cold.

There was a long silence as Hubbard took a few casual sips of his drink and seemed to regard Noah as an amusement.

This wasn't going at all like Noah imagined. This was a different screenplay altogether.

"You called the meeting," Hubbard said, playing more bored than bewildered. Certainly more bored than frightened. That wasn't a good sign.

"I want to talk about Thanh."

"How's he doing?" Zip asked with mock concern.

"I don't know. I haven't gotten any postcards from the hereafter."

Hubbard smiled. "Too bad. Anything else on your mind?"

"The cops think maybe I did it."

"Get a lawyer." Zip smiled. "See what a nice guy I am. Free advice at four in the morning."

"Word around town is that you're *not* a very nice guy."

"Well, sometimes rumors are true."

Hubbard moved toward the door. "Sorry I can't offer you a drink. It's late."

"Is it really that late?" Noah asked, looking at his watch.

"Time flies. Now I'm tired. And I'm asking you to go."

"And if I don't?" Noah said. "You'll call the police?"

"I could call your mother, but I don't know her."

"Maybe we can get a couple of homicide inspectors I know to come over and remove me."

"Maybe." He smiled. "If you mean Rose and Stern, I've talked to them. Told them how my houseboy just up and quit. That he'd been hanging around with a rough crowd, lately. That I was missing some jewelry, but hey! That's life. I can live without them. Oh, by the way, I was in Chile. Passport. Date and time stamped. So official."

This wasn't going at all well. Noah was at a loss. The plan, shoddy as it was, was shot. Noah hadn't put even the tiniest scare into Zip Hubbard. Who was this guy?

"His death means nothing to you?" Noah asked, trying to regroup or at least leave with some dignity.

Hubbard mimed lighting a match and tossing it. Noah wanted to hit him.

"You feel nothing?" Noah asked.

"I feel very tired. I've had quite an evening. Really very pleasant until now. I've got Jolie's number if you want it. Probably not tonight, though, right? You look awfully . . . tired. Get some rest." Hubbard opened the door. Noah had no more chips. The game was over. "I didn't catch your name, pal."

"No, you didn't."

72

"You must have had some sort of relationship with the kid, if they're tying you in. What kind of relationship was that?"

Noah started toward the door, thinking that his last statement was the only time he showed anything. A little jealousy maybe? His voice showed stress. It was as if something dawned on Zip — it was the tone a jealous man would use. Or just a naturally suspicious man.

"Would you like to know?" Noah baited.

"Nah, not really. A disposable little bitch, if you ask me."

Noah wasn't aware that he was going to hit Hubbard, until he saw the man, crashing to the floor.

"Don't get up," Noah said. "I guess we're both tired."

Noah drove down to Fillmore and sat in his car until dawn crept in. For a few moments, he wondered if he'd broken some bones in his hand. But all the fingers moved on command, despite the pain he felt in discovering the fact. Breakfast, then to his office. He'd crash until noon, at least, while clutching the cell phone he'd recently received from Olympia.

Brinkman was in the elevator when Noah arrived. The little white bag in the older detective's hand emitted a strong sweet cinnamon smell that enveloped the tiny, enclosed space.

"You're keeping some strange hours my boy — and some strange companions." There was no real derision in his voice, no real judging going on. It was his way of fishing for an explanation.

"You know a guy named Hubbard?"

"Should I?"

"From your police days?"

"Hubbard. There was an old Mother Hubbard somewhere in the back of my mind. Lost her mortgage, I think. There's a shopping center where her shoe used to be."

"This is one of mother's kids. Zip. Zip Hubbard."

"What are your dealings with him?" Brinkman asked, suddenly alert, suddenly interested.

"You know him?"

"Of him. About him. Regarding him. Enough of him to recommend that you keep your distance. Out of your league. Maybe even out of mine." Brinkman smiled.

"Why do they call him 'Zip'?"

"Because when Zip's assignment has been concluded someone has become zip. Nada. Nothing."

"Couple of more hints and I may get it."

"An enforcer. Hit man."

"What?" Noah said. "Why is he still running around?"

"All sorts of strange people running around. Where did you run into Zip?"

"A bar."

"A bar?"

"Initially."

"I hope you bought him a drink, told him your name was Dennis and that you were visiting from Tulsa."

"No, no, no. What do you think I am, Brinkman? An idiot? I punched his lights out."

"Perhaps I should have waited for the next elevator," Brinkman said and began to study the ceiling.

Noah figured this had to be his 1,913th miscalculation of human nature this month. Before, these little mistakes meant discomfort, embarrassment, or loss of income. They were rarely dangerous. This new knowledge about Zip Hubbard and his chosen vocation took the edge off the pleasure he'd gained by pissing him off and the sense of justice, however disproportional to the man's act, by knocking him in the head.

He paused at the door to his office *cum* abode as Brinkman made a hasty retreat to his. Noah could feel the hair rising on the back of his neck. Fresh scratches on the lock and the glimpse of raw wood on the doorframe suggested some serious tampering. All of it was of a small enough nature that he could easily have overlooked it, but he caught it; and this little event, following on the heels of Brinkman's revelation was more than frightening.

Putting a stakeout on a philandering husband was one thing. Assault and battery on a professional killer was something else entirely.

TEN

COULD HUBBARD HAVE learned of his identity and whereabouts so quickly? Noah could no longer call upon himself for such answers. He no longer trusted his own judgment. But he wasn't foolish enough to go barging in. On the other side could be a gun or a bomb. Or a cool-handed Zip.

No, he wasn't going in. What was the alternative? Call the police? The bomb squad? No, Brinkman. The fire escape ran from Brinkman's office, across an accountant's window, to Noah's place. There was a window.

"Brink my man," Noah said, trying to act nonchalant, nodding to and walking by Delores who was on the telephone speaking angrily in Spanish.

"Bad news," Brinkman said, looking up from a huge cinnamon roll. "I can tell it."

"I locked myself out of my office. I thought I'd use the fire escape."

"Why don't you take my gun," Brinkman said, opening a desk drawer.

"A gun?" Noah said.

"I saw you drive up, Noah. You can't fool a fooler. Your office key and your car key are on the same chain."

"Okay," Noah replied with a shrug. He reached for the gun.

Brinkman jerked it back. "On second thought, use this one," he said, leaning down and feeling for something under the desk. He came up with an old .32 and handed it to Noah. "Can't trace this one. I never saw it," he continued as he plucked a tissue from its box and wiped the weapon clean.

Noah checked the weapon to see if it was loaded. "This won't blow

75

up in my face?"

"What do you want for nothin'? A guarantee?" Brinkman asked, eyebrows raised. "But if you live, and don't shoot anybody, give it back."

"See you," Noah said, climbing through Brinkman's open window.

Noah heard the window shut and the lock on the window click back in place as he gained firm footing on the fire escape. He crept along, staying close to the building, trying to imagine if the sun would cast a shadow of him through the window before he could get there to take a careful glance. The morning light came from in front of him, casting the shadow back. Good, he thought.

He had no mirrors in his office to be careful of or, for that matter, use to his advantage. He slowed to inch-sized steps as he approached the window. He could see that it was unlocked. He couldn't tell whether he had left it that way or not. He locked the front door religiously, but often forgot the window.

At one edge now, Noah could peer in and see one quarter of the office. He could see the door to the storage room, the sofa and a bookcase. No human occupied his vision. Nothing seemed disturbed. A little farther and he could see most of his desk and the door to his office. Nothing. The door didn't look booby trapped. No wires or clocks or boxes of Acme dynamite.

Noah got down on his knees and crossed under the window. He needed to see the northside wall, the bathroom. Having made it to the other side of the window and then some, he stood and worked his way back. He could see the bathroom, most of it. All but a corner. What he could see was unoccupied. Nothing seemed out of place.

He lifted the window slowly and as quietly as he could. Two feet up from its base, the window stuck. Wouldn't budge. That was the way the window worked. He needed to jerk it up, at least past this point. He could never slide in the open space. He jerked suddenly and then, swept his body inside, all in one clumsy motion. He nearly fell. He searched the tiny bathroom. Nothing.

Noah looked around and then moved to the storage room. Nothing to do but to open it. That would be a good ploy, he thought. Scratch the front lock, something no pro would do, and then put the bomb on the second door. This was silly, he thought. Whoever it was, didn't get in.

That was all there was to it. Somebody tried to rob the place and gave up.

He took a deep breath and began to turn the knob — very slowly. He nudged the door open, also slowly. Suddenly there was an electronic beep.

"Shit," he jumped back. Another beep. Suddenly he realized it was the goddamned phone. With one sudden, angry move, he kicked the door open and jumped back to the side, falling on his butt.

Nothing. He got up slowly, gun ready. He jumped in with the .32 cocked. No one. Nothing other than the stack of boxes that had always been there.

Noah reached in his pocket for the cell phone. "Hello?" Nothing. "Hello?" Nothing.

He lost Olympia. Had to be her. And he lost her.

Suddenly his desk phone rang. He raced to it, tossing the .32 onto the sofa.

"Hello," an out of breath Noah said into the phone.

"You all right?"

"I'm in labor, but I have a few minutes before the baby pops out."

"I told you to keep the cell phone by you at all times," Olympia Rawley said.

"I did, but. . . ." As he talked, Noah went to the front door, opened it, peered both ways down the hallway. Empty.

"Don't talk, just listen. Be prepared," she said. He thought about the Boy Scouts. "Be ready at a moment's notice. Keep the next few days free for me. You understand?"

"Listen, I need to. . . ."

"Keep the phone on you. At all times!" she said crisply.

"Listen, I need. . . ."

Click.

"Goddamn you!" he said to the phone.

Then he remembered he had her number. The fact that she had to call him on his regular phone meant he had her number now.

"Gotcha bitch," he said, feeling guilty about the epithet, but smug about the catch. But, it seemed like every time Noah felt a little smug, as he had when he got to Hubbard before knowing who Hubbard was, and now with having gotten Olympia Rawley's phone number, something managed to wipe that little smart-aleck smile from his face.

This time that something was Stern and Rose.

"Told her, huh?" Stern said coming in the door.

"That wasn't nice. You need some sensitivity training," Rose chimed in.

"Hi guys," Noah said. "I didn't hear you knock."

"Oh damn," Rose said. He tugged on Sterns arm, pulling him back out of the office. They closed the door. They knocked.

"Come in," Noah said.

"See there," Rose said to Stern. Then to Noah. "I told him, but he didn't think you'd let us in, so he didn't see any reason to knock." He turned back to Stern. "See, you need to have more faith in human nature. Man is basically good. So you give him a chance."

"And if he screws up?" Stern said.

"Squish him like a bug."

"Squish?" Stern asked. That's a 'girl' word."

"Is not."

"Squish is a girl's word, Rose."

"Crush!" Rose yelled. "I meant to say crush."

"Glad you stopped by," Noah said.

"See there, Stern. Not only does he answer the door politely, but he's glad to see us."

"I know. I am ashamed."

"I wanted to talk with you," Noah said.

"We knew that," Rose said. "A message on our psychic hotline."

"I talked with a guy called 'Zip,'" Noah said.

"Why did you do that?" Stern asked.

"I figure since I didn't kill Thanh, somebody else must have."

"So you actually talked with Mr. Hubbard?" Rose asked, incredulous.

"I did."

Stern looked out of the window. Rose looked at the floor. The long silence that followed got to Noah first.

"I know. I mean I didn't know. That's why I talked with him. Now I know, I mean, about him. And I shouldn't have talked to him."

"Mmmmnnnnh," Stern said. He threw up his hands.

"He did it," Noah said. "Had to have. All but admitted it."

"All but?" Stern asked.

"Yeah."

"Mr. Hubbard has a very strong alibi," Stern said.

"Always does," Rose said.

"And you don't," Stern said. "Unless you come up with the married woman you mentioned earlier — you know the one in the RV?"

"I can, but you've got to give me time," Noah said.

"I guess we gotta, Stern. He says so."

He thought about calling her. He could wait. Waiting was a good idea. Maybe he should finish his search, though.

Stern took a seat.

"Lookin' for your alibi?" Rose said.

"A bomb or a microphone or something."

"I see," Stern said, raising his hand, finger circling his ear, making the "crazy" sign.

Rose shrugged.

"You lose the bomb or what?"

"Someone either broke in or tried to break in. My thoughts naturally led to your Mr. Zip. I don't think he likes me."

"I like you," Rose said. "Stern here likes you a little. Don't you Stern?"

"So tell me about your little chat with Hubbard," Stern said.

"Nothing much. I accused him of killing Thanh. He smiled, pretended like he was lighting a match, then said that according to his passport he was in Peru or something."

"Chile," Rose said.

A meticulous search yielded no bombs. Nothing was missing. He checked his phone to see if it had been bugged. He checked other likely places for microphones. None as far as he could tell.

"Now, can you relax?" Stern said.

"Yes."

"Let me repeat," Stern said. "He has an alibi. You don't."

"He probably did it," Rose said, "but we can't prove it."

"But me?"

"We can probably prove it."

"That's justice?" Noah asked.

"You act surprised," Rose said.

"We found traces of gasoline on your shirt. . . . " Stern said.

"I spilled some at the gas station when. . . ."

"No traces of carbon — smoke," Stern interrupted. He waited. "Dunno," he said.

"Dunno what?"

"Dunno what to do with you."

Noah noticed the gun was sitting on the sofa, in the crack. He went over and sat to hide it, hoped it would slip down inside between the back and the pillows.

"You've got a couple of days to talk to this woman, okay?" Stern asked and continued when Noah nodded his agreement. "It's not because we're nice guys, it's because we're just a little. . . ."

"Teensy weensy," Rose said.

". . . short on evidence."

"You know that Hubbard did it," Noah said. "He has motive. He was controlling and abusive according to the people on the street. . . ."

"The street? I'm impressed," Stern said.

". . . and my guess is that Thanh was leaving him or maybe the bastard was just jealous."

"Why would he be jealous of his house boy?" Stern asked

"House boy. You believe that?"

"You tell me what to believe."

"As I left he lost a little of his cool when he figured out I must have spent some time with Thanh."

"I'm listening," Stern said. "He was the jilted lover. You were the new love."

"No, well . . . that's what Hubbard thought. I'm not . . . oh fuck. You know the rest. The guy's a killer. A professional, I understand."

"You get around," Stern said.

"I'm impressed," Rose said, "but then I always was."

"I'd be more impressed," Stern said, standing up, "if our little private dick knew something about Hubbard's perfect alibi. Find somebody who can positively I.D. him on the date the fire was set."

"Shall we make him a deputy, Mr.Dillon?" Rose asked.

"You're right. Don't do anything, Lang. Not one damned thing. Jesus, I got carried away, didn't I?"

"You got excited. Who could blame you?" Rose said, with melodramatic compassion. "You've got a lot on your mind."

"I don't have anything on my mind."

"But that worries you, doesn't it?" Rose continued.

"I'm deeply depressed."

"And repressed," Rose said.

Stern nodded. "Rage. But maybe not as much as our Mr. Lang."

"Not me."

"You have motive, don't forget. Sudden surprise," Stern said. "Reach down and find a piece of gristle where there ain't supposed to be nothing. You go ballistic and in a macho rage you burn down the house. Motive. Opportunity. Gas can. No alibi."

"So what you're really saying is that I'm an easier bust than Hubbard?"

"We think you're a nicer guy," Rose said. "Doesn't that count for something?"

By afternoon, a helpless feeling swept over him. There was nothing he could do. Regarding the ruthless Mr. Hubbard, Noah's best strategy was to stay as invisible to the man as possible. As far as Olympia was concerned, he could do nothing about finding Charles Rawley until he heard from her. He'd exhausted his search. All he had was one poor man — Morcham — who lost a hand through some as yet unexplained event shortly after publishing a nasty book on the tycoon and shortly before another nasty book was in preparation. But what did that give him?

He remembered the money, went to the chair where he'd stuffed it. He pulled it out. All there. Most of the afternoon went quickly as he snored away on the sofa. At five, he turned on the news and watched television until eight when hunger began to gnaw at him.

Noah called out for a pizza. An hour later, a restless P.I. was ready to call and cancel, go out, get loaded. No, the moment he became a stumbling slob, Olympia would call or he'd run into Zip. Hell, he had money now, at least enough to coast through a few months and perhaps more on the way. Then why wasn't he any happier? He felt bad about Thanh. But it was over. Done.

A knock on the office door.

"Be right there." He opened the door, reached in his back pocket for his wallet.

There was a young Asian guy with some sort of flat top or Mohawk or something and an earring.

"Where's the pizza?" Noah asked.

"I didn't know you wanted one."

"What? Oh my God! Thanh."

"I'm sorry," he said. "I had nowhere else to go."

ELEVEN

NOAH GRABBED HIS arm, pulled him in and, after glancing into the hallway, shut the door.

"I'm sorry," Thanh said.

"My God!"

"I look funny, I know."

"No, you're fine." He looked different — not just the hair cut. That in itself was a jolt. But the demeanor was different. Sober. The light in his eyes had dimmed. "I'm just confused," Noah said. "But I'm happy. I thought you were dead?"

"Was it in the papers?"

"I don't know." Noah thought about telling him about the problem with the police. He decided he wouldn't. "First, tell me what happened. No, first sit down."

"I was doing my laundry," Thanh said, sitting on the sofa. "I forgot my jeans and I came back to the building. I couldn't get in. Fire trucks, ambulances, flashing lights. People running around hysterically in this huge crowd. I didn't know what to do. They wouldn't let me in the building. I looked around for my friend, but couldn't find him."

"He was the one who died?" Noah asked.

"Yes. He wasn't supposed to." Thanh looked so sad Noah wanted to put his arms around him, but couldn't. "It was supposed to be me."

"I know."

"You know?"

"I figured it out. Let's talk about all of that later. Where have you been?"

"Hiding. I heard the police at the scene talking to the firemen. Someone set it. And when I discovered 507C was one of the. . . . well I knew. I got down to Daly City, stayed with a hairdresser I used to know. It didn't work. Me staying, I mean."

"Sit down. Let me get you a Coke." Thanh didn't object. Noah's short mission to the little refrigerator was interrupted by another knock.

Noah was pleased by the first surprise visitor, but he wasn't sure he wanted to be surprised again.

Thanh looked nervously at the door. Noah motioned for him to go into the storage room and waited until the door was shut. He took the gun from beneath the sofa cushion and went to the door, keeping his body against the wall as he reached over to open the door.

On the other side was a young man holding a flat white box.

"This is crazy," Noah said, shoving his newfound toy down his back, between his belt and tee shirt. "Hi."

"You ordered a pizza, right?" the kid asked, obviously confused by the armed reception.

"Yes, I most certainly did. I just wanted to make sure it wasn't from Dominos."

The kid shook his head, more bored than frightened.

"Just a moment." Noah gave the kid a twenty and told him he could keep the change. Noah slipped the gun back into its hiding place and opened the door for Thanh.

"Pizza," he said to Thanh. "Just pizza."

Thanh took a deep breath, tried to smile.

"Hubbard doesn't know you're alive, does he?"

"How do you know about him?"

"I've been more involved in your life than you might imagine."

"I don't understand."

"When was the last time you had something to eat?"

"It doesn't matter."

"Eat some pizza. Now about those Cokes."

Thanh sat at the desk, Noah on the sofa, noticing that after Thanh's initial denial of hunger, he was doing a pretty good job on the pie. After ten minutes of quiet and determined eating, Noah broke the silence.

"How long were you with him?"

Thanh looked surprised. "What?"

"With Hubbard."

"You didn't tell me how you knew."

"I asked around."

"Four years."

"Four?"

Thanh nodded.

"I paid him a visit."

"What?" Thanh asked, surprised or upset, or both.

"He doesn't know who I am — and he thinks you're dead. So we're fine, I think. He said you were his house boy."

"I was. That's what I became," Thanh said, getting up and going into the bathroom. Noah heard the water running. "At first I was his lover. In the end, I was his houseboy. These things happen."

"What did happen?"

"Things changed, that's all." Thanh went to the window now, his finger outlining the frame that enclosed the glass.

"You don't want to talk about it," Noah said. "It's all right."

He looked at Noah, pleading. "I don't have to be there anymore. It's past. It's gone. Over." His hand went to sweep back hair that wasn't there anymore. A forced, but nonetheless pleasant smile. "Do I look terrible?"

"No, no. You look fine." He almost said "more like a boy." He was glad he stopped when he had. He was wandering around in unfamiliar psychological territory.

Thanh went into the bath again. Noah was pretty sure the visits were to glance in the mirror.

"I have a favor to ask," Thanh said, coming out of the bath again.

"Okay."

"I don't have any place to go."

"You stay here then." Noah surprised himself.

"As long as he thinks I'm dead. . . ."

"I know."

"Just for a little while, until. . . ."

"You've already closed the sale, Thanh. You stay."

"Really?" Thanh asked, showing the first trace of his old smile. "Oh God, thank you." It was Thanh who resisted the urge to hug. It was visible. "I'll be good."

"Don't thank me yet . . . I have a selfish motive."

"What?" A little bit more of a smile.

"Not that. I mean . . . the police. They think I did it."

"That you did what?"

"Killed you."

"Oh . . .You want me to talk to the police? I don't want you to be in trouble because of me."

"Let's talk about all of that later. We'll work it out. Just one more question. Did you try to get in here earlier, play around with the lock."

"Yes," Thanh said. "I'm sorry."

"No, I'm glad it was you. It means we have some time."

Noah could feel the tension, but he couldn't figure out the cause. He didn't ask because he wasn't sure he wanted to know. Thanh was alive. He was alive. That was good enough for now.

In the storage room, the two of them rearranged boxes. Boxes of old clothes formed the base for a bed. An old clip-on light was attached to a pipe to give Thanh a little light in the windowless room.

"What is this?" Thanh asked, as he rummaged through an open box.

"My life."

"No, this. Pink Floyd."

"Music of my youth."

"Pink Floyd," Thanh said again and laughed.

"Surely you know Pink Floyd. Dark Side of the Moon."

"Who's this?"

It was a photograph slid between the back of the album and the clear plastic cover.

"Sarah. My wife. Former wife."

"What happened to her?"

"Went away."

"I shouldn't ask."

"She went away, Thanh. That's. . . ."

"Okay."

The two of them were an odd pair, Noah thought. So far, little more than two surfaces — oddly attracted to each — came into contact for whatever reason. Whatever was beneath or behind those surfaces, Noah thought, remained there.

"She went away in her mind and then she went away altogether." Noah sat on one of the boxes. "Why don't you tell me what I don't know."

"What?"

"What went on with you and Hubbard? He beat you?"

"How did you know about that?"

"I talked to some people. Why didn't you go to the police?"

"I'm not legal," Thanh said.

"That's the only reason?"

"No, but that's enough. They'd ship me somewhere. I don't know where. I don't want to be sent off again?"

"You're not telling me everything."

"I'm telling you what you are able to understand."

"You think I'm that dumb?"

"You and I don't live in the same world."

"We don't, I'm sure."

"No. When you have no money, people don't have to respect you. When you are of mixed race, you are not trusted by anyone. Then, when you are like me — a ladyboy or whatever you want to call me — you have no identity. People see you as a freak, an accident. The authorities, the police, see you as abnormal. Nature has already made you an outlaw. And that gives everyone the right to hate you. To hurt you. This is the truth. I have no standing, anywhere."

"I'm sorry."

"Why? I'm not sorry."

"I mean it hasn't been easy."

"No one has it easy. I faced those facts about who I am. And I have chosen not to pretend to be someone else. Unfair or not, I know the consequences. And I have to act accordingly. People who don't know can't. . . ."

"I understand."

"Be glad that you don't." He said it firmly. Then his face softened a bit. "I'm very happy that you don't and I am very grateful to you for your help." He smiled. "It hasn't been easy for you." He took a breath. "Anyway, let's think of something nice. Tell me a story. Tell me about a time when you were the most happiest of all."

The sun abandoned Noah as he climbed up a long and narrow stair into a room with a low ceiling, a room filled with more shadow than light. People were asleep on the floor amidst clumps of clothing and twisted blankets. A sound came from somewhere. The sound was foreign, deep and full of sorrow. It haunted and frightened him. A call from a distance— perhaps out in the universe somewhere.

The sound lifted him from his sleep, from his dream and into a familiar blackness. Eyes open, he recognized the feel of his sofa and the different rectangle of black that was the window into the real night. Was it real? The sound again. From the storage room.

Noah rummaged in the darkness to his desk and into the drawer for the flashlight. Inside, he flashed the beam on the sleeping form. Thanh, his nakedness glistening with perspiration. Now the sound again. Noah switched on the rigged light and gently shook the sleeper.

"You okay?" Noah asked.

For a moment Thanh was terrified. Eyes wide, mouth agape. Suddenly his face softened. He took a deep breath. "Oh, Noah." All of the fear seemed to leave him. His face took on a soft and dreamy countenance. Thanh smiled briefly and turned over, pulling the blanket up over him.

"I'll get you a towel. You're soaked."

He had towels. He could use them as sheets. "You'll have to get up a minute," Noah said. "let me change those."

"It's all right."

"No, it's not," Noah put his hand on Thanh's forehead. "You're all right now. You must have had a fever and it broke. You've got to get out of those wet sheets."

"I must have been dreaming," Thanh said, sliding naked out of bed.

Noah dried Thanh's face and shoulders then, realizing the scope of the operation, smiled and handed the towel to Thanh and searched for something to cover him. He found an old, battered wool shirt.

"Put this on until I get dry sheets on here." Noah bundled the wet sheets and tossed them aside. He put on a new ones, felt the blanket. It was dry enough. Again, he was glad he had done the laundry.

"It's soft," Thanh said, feeling the material of the shirt. "Smells good."

"Okay, get back in. I'm going to get you some aspirin and some water."

"I'm sorry."

"No more sorrys. What were you dreaming about?"

"I don't know." He smiled at Noah whose doubtful face betrayed him. "I don't. Honest. Must have been something horrible, waking you up like that."

"It's nothing. I have trouble waking up, not going to sleep," he lied. "I'll be fine."

Thanh climbed back into bed, turned out the light. "Life takes funny turns, doesn't it?" he asked.

Noah stood in the thin band of light from the other room, a streak leaking into this darkness. He thought about answering. He didn't know what to say and whatever he might have said, he knew it wouldn't come out right. The accidental physical intimacy he shared on that first night, aside, he had become closer to this strange stranger than he had with anyone in a dozen years. There was nothing wrong with that, he thought. This, whatever it was, was new.

"Funny turns indeed," he managed to utter as he shut the door.

He talked Thanh into staying in the makeshift bed most of the next day. Telling him not to answer the door or the phone, Noah went out to get soup, crackers and juice and returned with something chicken and noodlish in a Styrofoam cup, a box of saltines, orange juice and Ginger Ale. Not exactly well practiced in the art of nurturing, he remembered these were the things his mother had given him when he was sick and feverish.

Later, he made tea and cinnamon toast. Thanh napped. Noah developed a headache from too much TV. The day wouldn't end. Again, it was difficult for Noah to tell how much or how little he had slept.

Sometime between nightmares and the next morning, the rains began. If Noah dreamed in that interim, he recalled nothing. Even so, when he awoke, he possessed a sense of uneasiness, a vague fear that was bone deep. He was on the verge — of what he didn't know. On the verge of something. He didn't get up. He stayed, almost hidden in the scratchy wool blanket, looking at the gray light seeping in the window.

Noah heard the door to the storage room open. He closed his eyes — then let them open in what he hoped would be an undetectable squint. He wasn't ready for conversation or for the day to begin. He wanted to retreat to dreamless sleep. He saw Thanh tiptoe across the room to the bathroom. On Thanh's smaller, slenderer body, the flannel shirt looked like a robe. A woman. A child. It was difficult to see Thanh as an adult male. But he was, wasn't he?

The wind picked up and Noah could hear the patter of the rain against the window. Sleep must have overtaken him. He didn't hear Thanh return. The next sensation was the smell of coffee.

"What time is it?" Noah asked.

"Nine."

"Damn."

"You have an appointment?" Thanh asked with concern.

Noah laughed. "No. It doesn't matter, does it?" He got up, looked around for his shoes. "I like to be presentable by eight, you know, for the parade of new clients."

"You have clients now?" Thanh said, handing Noah a cup.

"Actually I do. One. But the whole thing is very secret," Noah went to the window, looked out. "I don't even know. Grisly out there in the world today. Wet and grisly." He turned toward Thanh. "Do you think he'd recognize you with your hair cut?"

Thanh shrugged. Perhaps he didn't want to talk about it, Noah thought. But they'd have to. Eventually, Thanh would have to go out.

"Maybe we can get you some different clothes. A flannel shirt that fits. Butch it up. Some loose jeans. Boots."

Thanh smiled. "I'll look like a lesbian."

"It is confusing," Noah said, unsuccessfully holding back a smile. "But the whole world. . . ." The sentence trailed off.

"What?"

"Everything is confusing." Noah meant it. Everything.

The phone beeped. He began to look among his bedclothes. Thanh found it, handed it to Noah.

"Olympia," he said.

"I need you tonight. Late probably. . . ."

"Listen this time goddamit," he told her, "I'm not doing another fucking thing for you until you answer some questions. You got it?"

"I do," Olympia said, calmly. "Go ahead. But make it brief. And don't mention names. You understand?"

"All right." The name not to mention was 'Rawley.' "I went to the boat. An old man was there. Said he owned it. Went back. Wasn't even your dock. . . ."

"I know," she said, a bit of compassion in her voice. "My father is protective. He knows the dangers I face from kidnappers. I think the situation I'm in reinforces that notion, don't you?"

"True. But. . . ."

"I don't know if you can believe me. I hope you do whether you can understand this or not, I am frightened for my husband. I'm frightened for me. Tonight. . . ."

"Does your husband handle critics by cutting off their hands?" Noah blurted. He hadn't planned to ask her that. The idea that he might be working for the wrong side had just bubbled up from somewhere. It was obviously troubling him, despite the fact that he hadn't given much thought to those kinds of issues in a long time.

"I have no idea what you're talking about. What's going on?"

"Too much smoke and too many mirrors," he said.

"Are you with me or not?"

"Listen."

"I need to know. Don't do this to me now. You can't wait until I'm desperate. I've counted on you. It's too late, too late, Noah." She wasn't crying or even about to, but he heard the stress in her voice. She was pleading. "Don't do this to me. There's no place for me to go."

"All right."

"Are you with me? Please say 'yes.'"

"All right."

"I need to hear the word, 'yes,' Noah."

"Yes." He couldn't get the resentment out of his voice.

"Stay by the phone. Tonight."

There was the now familiar click.

"Damn," Noah said, clicking the off button and tossing the phone on the sofa.

"Everything okay?" Thanh asked, his face showing genuine concern.

TWELVE

After a long conversation with Thanh, Noah called Inspector Rose.

"Why hello there, Mr. Lang! It's great to hear from you, but we generally like to take confessions in the office."

"Only if you have the little booths."

"We can arrange a booth. The governor has a quiet little room at the prison he's fond of for guests like you."

"What I called to tell you about was. . . well you know the fellow I was supposed to have murdered?"

"What a surprise. You're calling me to tell me you didn't kill him?"

"No. Better. I'm telling you he's not dead."

"Now, there's an alibi I haven't heard in awhile. That's a good one." A muffled voice: "Lang. Says Sasha's alive." Momentarily, the voice returned to full volume. "Stern says you're improving with practice. Now you're not going to tell me he went off in the Gypsy Caravan, are you?"

"Yep."

"I see."

"Thanh's blood type is B negative."

"And?"

"Check the victim's blood type, that's all I can say."

"Pretty clever, Mr. Lang. You make up a rare blood type and we try to match it to the body."

"Inspector Rose?"

"Yes."

"Check with California Pacific Medical Center. Thanh had an accident courtesy of your friend, Zip Hubbard. As a result Thanh required a transfusion. All of this happened less than a year ago. Oh, and by the way, he was treated at the same hospital for a broken left wrist. You can check both of those against your victim's corpse, inspector. It's not Thanh."

There was silence.

"I can have my lawyer do this and contact the District Attorney."

"We'll check," Rose said soberly.

"One more thing. If your friend, Zip, knows this fact, Thanh will be in serious danger."

"Good day, Mr. Lang. We'll be in touch, so you be in touch."

Thanh spent the afternoon and evening on the sofa, alternately watching television and sleeping. It was nail-biting time for Noah. It was like waiting at the airport for a flight that was already an hour late. He tried watching television, but couldn't concentrate. He did, however, read more of Morcham's *Collateral Damage*. Parts of it were riveting enough to take his mind off the slow pace time had begun to take.

> Basically, Charles Rawley is nearing greatness. He now has the capability to terrorize world economic markets, to buy and sell small governments and to manipulate large ones. Through his holdings, he can control the content and dissemination of information. These are the tools of the 21st Century Alexander the Great.
>
> Surely, he is not the only powerful businessman. But he is one of the few most powerful. One thinks of a Bill Gates and even if one can comprehend the tremendous wealth and subsequent power of such an accumulation of wealth and market dominance, you are talking about a lucky kid facing a person of equal financial power, but with the personality of a predator created in Hell's Kitchen. Gates, his economic kin and their "revenge of the nerds" form a toothless army. They are extremely easy prey for the likes of Charles Rawley.
>
> Hell's Kitchen is no exaggeration. Power by intimidation is standard operation for Rawley. Though based on rumors, the stories of Rawley's own international, expertly trained covert forces are more than likely true. From separate, reliable sources, the stories about his willingness to use force when his more subtle means fall short, are true.
>
> The tentacles of his organization have curled around the

globe and its increasingly interdependent economy, especially third world economies viewed for future exploitation, where the rule of force is all that is understood. Rawley understands it well. If even half the reports that have come my way are true, the Mafia looks like Spanky and our Gang.

Noah went to the window, stared out into the gray, interrupted only by the harsh architecture of the industrial buildings. He wasn't sure when afternoon turned into evening and evening into night. But it had. Thanh was still asleep, breathing more easily. Noah covered the sleeper's bare shoulder.

Noah sat at the desk, picked up the book and opened it randomly:

> What we can expect now is a whole new series of mergers, by and large, reinstating the reverses powerful businesses faced in previous decades when antitrust was effective. You will again see monstrous banks, huge oil corporations, giant communications conglomerates. They will advance the neo-feudal system that will take charge of the global economy and render most of the world's population as employee-peasants. No one, including — perhaps especially — the peasant will have a clue. The new order, by then, will have become institutionalized.
>
> Because the communication systems are in the hands of neo-feudal proponents, most people won't even know what is happening to them. Not only will adults be lulled into acceptance by the all pervasive "tube," children will get early doses of this ideology masquerading as free market capitalism, in the new "privatized" school system. And if they fail to grasp the ideology of privatization, they may find themselves in one of the new privatized prisons.
>
> Charles Rawley not only understands all of this, he is prophet, producer and protector of the movement — a movement he hopes ultimately to control. And given his ever-increasing power, he may very well reach his goal unless his enemies prevail. And of course, the longer they wait, the more difficult it will be to keep Rawley from achieving what he perceives to be his destiny.

Whew! Noah put the book down. He couldn't make up his mind if Morcham was just another crackpot conspiracy theorist or had discovered unholy truths about how the world was unfolding. Was nothing as it seemed? Was there always something underlying what was under-lying . . . ?

Who was he working for? Would he know after tonight?

The phone call came at 11:15. By that time, Noah had long abandoned *Collateral Damage* and the menacing Charles Rawley. The television was on, but it might as well have been an "exit" sign. Noah wasn't even aware of what he was watching or what he was thinking. He was a head of cabbage.

The beeping, though he expected it, shook him. It was Olympia.

"At midnight, you will be at Roose Warehouse near China Basin Boulevard and Central Basin. Go early, you'll find it. You will be met at the gate. Someone will take you where you need to go. What you'll do is meet Charles. If he's alive and well, you'll call me."

"How do I do that?" Noah asked, not wanting her to know he had her phone number.

"The cell phone I gave you? Push the pound sign and then 999. It's programmed to dial me. Right away. In the presence of Charles. I re-peat, do not dial the number until you are with Charles. The number only works once. Do you understand?"

"Yes." He wasn't sure he understood. Only works once? But her voice was hurried and impatient and he was too angry with her and too aware of Sasha being in the room to think clearly.

"Do not do anything else. If you follow directions, you will receive $20,000 in cash within the week. Do you understand?"

"Where at the warehouse?"

"There's a main gate."

"Is that where they're holding him?"

"I don't know. Probably not. Any problem with the instructions?"

"No."

"All right."

"Why so much money?"

"Could be dangerous, Noah. Take care."

Click.

Noah threw the phone toward the sofa, then realized what he'd done.

If he'd broken it. . . .

"Oh God," he said, shaking his head. "I'm an idiot."

"You're a very nice idiot, if you ask me," Thanh said, letting his face remain sober for a moment, then letting the grin take over. "Can I help?"

"No," Noah said, putting on his shoes. "Listen. There's uh . . . a chance . . . um . . . some uncertainty about what I'm doing. I mean tonight. You just don't know about these things." He knew he wasn't making much sense. He decided to just say it. "There's money in the seat of the chair." Noah pointed to the desk chair. "It's enough to get you started. . . ."

"What are you saying?" Thanh said.

"I'm saying . . . just in case." He put his hands up to stop Thanh from talking. He could tell by the look on his face an objection was on its way. Noah looked away. " If I'm not back by daylight . . . start thinking about where you want to go." Noah caught another glimpse of Thanh's expression. To avoid the look, he began checking pockets for his car keys and talking to the wall. "You probably need to do it by bus, because the airlines demand an I.D. Get over to Oakland and grab a Greyhound. Go to New York, some place where you can be absorbed into the culture, where he can't find you. Change your name."

"Noah," Thanh said and then nothing else.

In the alley heading toward his car, Noah felt cold. He hoped he wasn't coming down with what Thanh had, though he suspected Thanh's illness was as much exhaustion as anything else. In any event, he should have worn a warmer jacket. He had put on a windbreaker, Brinkman's pistol in one pocket, weighing it and him down on one side. A small, light, cellular phone in the other pocket, not balancing the weight at all.

The destination? He knew the area, roughly. He was pretty sure he knew the warehouse. If there were an undeveloped inch of San Francisco, it was there along the bay from China Basin to Hunter's Point. In some places, it was a no-man's land. Little if any good existed in these parts. He turned on the heat as his little Alfa Romeo made its way to Third Street.

What in the hell was going on? He'd never had a job where he'd been kept so much in the dark. But poverty has a way of making you irresponsible. And apparently stupid. If Olympia wanted to make sure

96

her husband was alive, wouldn't a phone call have sufficed? It certainly would be cheaper. And what would prevent the kidnappers from pulling the plug on Charles Rawley once his identification was confirmed to Olympia? Noah wasn't bringing anything to this little party but himself.

A pawn. Clearly a fool. Doubly so. He couldn't help but think that Thanh and the money would be gone when he got back. The temptation would be too great. Thanh feared for his life, needed more than anything to make a new one. What would he do if he were in Thanh's shoes? He couldn't blame him. It's only money. "Easy come, easy go," he said to himself and wished that it was daylight. Charles Rawley or not, that area of the city was dangerous.

Mist gathered on the windshield. Noah turned on the wipers. Dark, cold and unfamiliar territory. What was new? Not only did he not know what in the hell this was all about, he could make no better sense out of his life.

There they were, no doubt. Three cars pulled in front of a tall chain link fence by a gate. A small, worn sign said, "Roose Warehouse, Main Gate."

Six guys got out of the cars as Noah pulled up. They were suits, men in dark suits and overcoats carrying flashlights. He pulled his pistol from his pocket and tucked it under the seat. Otherwise, he'd surely lose it.

"Turn your lights off," said a voice from the approaching pack.

Just before he pushed the little button, Noah noticed their faces were all fuzzy, indistinct. No faces. . . .

THIRTEEN

IT NOW DAWNED on him — as he placed himself in the hands of escapees from the X-Files — that despite the sense of foreboding he'd felt when he first met the tycoon's wife — this was far worse than he had imagined. This was deep shit.

In addition to not trusting others, he didn't know what part of himself to trust anymore. Picking up a little number named Sasha one night led to a confusing momentary but no less profound sexual experience or not and to a very nasty professional murderer. Foolishly accepting this implausible case from a client named Olympia didn't add to his self confidence.

The only good thing that crossed the synapses of his confused mind was that these goons felt the need to wear a disguise — in this case nylon stockings pulled down over and distorting their faces— which meant, he hoped, they weren't going to kill him. Nobody worries about a dead eyewitness.

"You know if you guys want to save some money, buy some panty hose and split them," Noah said, as his jacket was being removed. One of the guys took the telephone and tossed it into the Alfa Romeo.

"I need that," Noah said.

No one acknowledged his need. His body was being unlovingly caressed by two sets of hands. Hands went into his pockets. Contents removed. While one of the six ran a metal rod over Noah's body, another had lifted his wallet and taken it back to one of the big black cars. Now his shoes were being removed and tossed into the car. They were obviously searching for more than weapons. He watched as one of them locked his car. Thorough, responsible kidnappers, Noah thought.

They were also interchangeable — dressed in dark clothing, feature-less faces, quiet. They checked his ears, his hair, removed his belt. One of them held Noah's head in place, while another opened his jaw. They were checking his mouth. He could feel the cold metal of a smaller flashlight, next the sharper touch of something probing inside his mouth — pressing against his fillings. Still no one spoke.

Done with the dental investigation and his head returned to his own power, Noah looked around. A huge, gothic structure stood silhouetted against the only slightly lighter sky. There were no cars on the road. Noah wondered why. Just because it was late?

The man who took his wallet was still in the automobile. He was talking on the phone. That was the last thing he saw before one of the faceless goons slipped a hood over Noah's head. He felt the arms of two others guiding him along the crumbling asphalt of the street until he was shoved into the backseat of one of the sedans. He wasn't treated roughly, but firmly. Clearly, these guys had instructions. Clearly, they weren't recruited from a temp agency. The car started. He felt the movement. It was obvious they were leaving the Roose Warehouse — as well as Noah's car, shoes, jacket, gun and telephone — behind.

Noah turned to the seat mate on his right, "Where are we going?" Nothing. "Now if someone would just cover his ears we could do the 'hear no evil, see no evil, speak no evil thing'. . . ." His sense of humor wasn't appreciated, apparently, and Noah decided to shut up. No one else spoke either. No threats, no reassurance on the ride to somewhere.

Within five minutes, he felt the car turn. He could hear the sound of gravel crackle under the tires. In 30 seconds the car stopped. He heard at least one other car come to a stop as well. Car doors opened, shut. His car door too. He was pulled out into the cold dampness again and led, in his stockinged feet, over an expanse of sharp edged gravel.

There was a knocking sound and the sound of a bolt sliding out of, or into place. A creak of a door. Then another.

First voice of the evening.

"There are four steep steps. You're at the base now. Please proceed."

The steps were metal. Noah could feel the cold dampness through his thin socks just as he could feel the wood after the fourth step. He was inside. The wind and the damp had stopped and the atmosphere was warm and stuffy. Cigarette smoke. Liquor. Maybe wine.

"Noah Lang, private investigator," a voice said.

The hood was removed.

Noah was inside a semi trailer. It wasn't hard to figure out — and he'd been inside a few before. The only light came from a bare bulb fixed on the ceiling casting a dim luminescence on the wood-lined interior.

The one cheap bulb illuminated Charles Rawley. The photographs in the various books and articles and the one Olympia gave to Noah may have reflected how light bounced off bones and flesh. They did not carry how impressive he was in person. Sitting on a metal chair amidst boxes in the crummy decor of a semi trailer, Charles Rawley, wearing black jeans and a black sweatshirt, looked like a general.

At the moment, the general was thumbing through Noah's wallet. Charles Rawley was not a captive as Olympia had said. Charles Rawley was in control.

"You were supposed to bring papers."

"Those weren't my instructions. I was supposed to verify your identity — find out if you were unharmed and still alive."

The man smiled, but there was nothing kind in it. He turned to one of the guys, "Get her on the phone. Scramble it first." He had no more interest in Noah Lang.

One man was by the double doors near the exit. Another was punching some numbers into a cell phone. A third stood behind Charles Rawley. A fourth may have been outside. Noah remembered there were six. Where were the other two?

"Nora?" Rawley said after one of his minions handed him the phone. "Hello honey, we had a deal, didn't we?" Rawley's face was passive, showing no sign of concern. But something had obviously gone wrong. "You send me a delivery boy minus the delivery. What do you think is going to happen to you people?" He listened. "Yes. He's here," Rawley said, his voice still steady, his eyes dismissing the delivery boy. "Standing right in front of me, empty handed."

"Empty headed," Noah volunteered.

"I don't want to spend the rest of the evening on the telephone with you. We had an arrangement. You decided to play games. You must know this will cost you?" He listened. The only emotion that crossed his face was a look of boredom. "No, no, no, sweetheart. What are you going to do?"

Noah listened.

"The time frame is too long. Your costs escalate by the hour." Rawley paused. "Not just financial. Human too." A thin smile crossed his face.

Noah thought he heard some sort of strange rumbling. Outside. It took him a second to realize that it was a sound familiar to him from his days on an aircraft carrier. No doubt in his mind. A chopper approached.

"Shit," Noah said under his breath. Maybe Rawley didn't know why Noah was sent, but Noah suddenly knew. He was an unwitting kamikaze.

He looked toward the huge double doors. They weren't latched, but there was a faceless man standing there, arms folded.

With only a fraction of a second of thought, Noah smashed his fist into the bulb above him, dodged to one side in the darkness, then angled at the spot where the door was supposed to be and flung his body at it. Either he'd hit the man guarding the doors or he'd hit the doors directly. He felt the soft whoosh of hitting a man in the midsection. The momentum barely slowed and he felt the cushioning effect of the man hitting the door. The doors opened, banging back against the truck. Noah's body overshot the guard's whose now limp form was half on the metal steps and half on the gravel. Noah himself felt the coarse gravel eat up his clothing and dig into his flesh — though in fact he forced his body to roll in the direction he was already heading. The sound of the helicopter was loud and getting louder. Noah's roll on the gravel finally ended and he was on his feet, running, painfully — barefooted on the gravel — as far away from the truck as possible.

He didn't look back. He kept running, his quick body part inventory suggested nothing was broken. Bruised for sure, he wondered however how much of his body was bleeding. He wondered whether or not a hired goon or a speeding bullet would cut him down before he could get out of range.

For a split second the sky was lit, lighter than noon, and he felt something — like the hand of God — push him to the ground just as the horrendous sound of the explosion obliterated all senses. For a moment, he knew nothing, felt nothing, except a heartbeat that threatened to come crashing through his ribcage, saw nothing except pure white before pure black set in.

Consciousness came to him gradually. He was able to get to his feet before he even understood who he was, let alone where. He looked around, disoriented. All he could remember was noise and light. In front of him, there was neither. Only darkness. Peripherally his eyes caught little flashes of light and a horrible smell. Sulfur? He couldn't be sure. He turned. There was a car in flames. There was a form, perhaps a body also in flames, midway between him and the flaming automobile.

Noah felt lost. Maybe he'd died and his soul was dropped into limbo. Then he remembered the trailer. It was gone. Completely gone. He felt water dripping on his hand. He looked down and saw blood. It was coming back now. His escape. Charles Rawley. The phone call. The sound of the helicopter. He had a car somewhere. But he didn't know where. He wasn't even sure where he was.

What should he do? He still had trouble thinking. What he should do next kept receding in his brain as thoughts about Olympia setting him up took over. What a piece of work she was. He'd have to save her for later. His survival was the priority of the moment.

He had to think. He was the only one to escape. Rawley surely didn't. Neither did the others. They killed Rawley. They, whoever they were, probably thought Noah was dead as well. For the moment, he thought, that was good. They not only thought Noah was dead; it was, in fact, their intention. The most obvious problem at the moment was getting the hell out of there before the police arrived. He didn't want any conversations with them before he had a chance to sort all of this out himself. The next problem was to find a way home to tend to his wounds and get some sleep.

"Okay," he thought, limping out to the street. He was pretty sure the car had gone straight from the warehouse to this truck trailer office. The only turn was to the right. What did that do in terms of figuring out which way to his car? This wasn't too difficult. Since the San Francisco Bay was on one side of the property, that meant the goons' car could only have come from one direction in order to make a right turn.

That meant he would turn left. A less than five-minute drive at 20 or

30 miles an hour meant that he had traveled roughly. . . . what? "Come on brain." This is elementary mathematics. "Figure it out." Should be less than three or four miles. That was a long way without shoes in the middle of a cold, wet night, but it was a helluva lot better than if it had been a 30-minute drive. He could do it.

Fortunately both legs worked. As the shock wore off, the pain of the abrasions added a sharpness to the dull ache of his bones. He would be in more pain tomorrow, in places he couldn't even imagine. For now he could walk and his most pressing problem was whether or not he was heading in the right direction.

FOURTEEN

By the time Noah reached his car, daylight showed itself in a thin strip of pearl at the base of the horizon. Dizziness and nausea plagued him over a distance that was greater than he imagined. On a trek that he could only hope led to his little car, he had to rest more and more frequently and for longer and longer duration.

The occasional car didn't stop. No doubt he looked like any of thousands of homeless that occupied the city streets as he wandered drunken-like and unstable in the night and early morning. Eventually he made it. One goal met, he slid down the side of his Alfa Romeo to rest before he undertook the next leg of his trip. He thought maybe he had dozed, butt on the ground, body resting against the car, his whole being too beat up and worn out to do much else. He had no idea how long he'd been there. But it was a more definite dawn when he regained a sense of consciousness. The goons had locked the doors to his car. How kind, Noah thought. Noah nodded — as a drunk might — to an imaginary friend. "Thank you for your consideration."

He pounded his fist against the window. The glass vibrated under his weak attempt. But the shock to Noah must have aroused his brain. Even if he had the strength, there was no need to slice his hand and arm. Fortunately, the area had plenty of rocks, bricks and other debris. He picked up a piece of concrete and smashed the window.

He sat for awhile behind the wheel, weak and unmotivated. Slowly, some measure of strength returned, but he found that hot-wiring the car was much more difficult than it should have been because his right hand wouldn't cooperate and kept dripping blood on the wiring. However, his experience reclaiming hot new Corvettes for angry finance companies came in handy and he was able to ignite the engine and drive back to his office in the light traffic of early morning.

It hadn't occurred to him, however, until he saw the front door of the building that he had absolutely no way of getting in. His office keys, like the others, were in some dead man's pocket if there was anything left that resembled a man or a pocket. Noah leaned his head back and the next thing he knew the puzzled face of Barry Brinkman was coming into focus.

"Rough night, eh, old boy?"

"What time is it?"

"Nine."

"Shit," he said.

"Are you in any immediate danger of death?"

"I'm fine. Lovely of you to ask."

"I'd walk you up, but two things prevent it. One is that I'm not going up. The second is that I really don't like the idea of being seen with you. Seems as though old Zippety Doo Dah is looking for you."

"What?"

"Zip. The hit man you assaulted."

Noah nearly knocked Brinkman over, getting out of the Alfa Romeo. He began running toward the building.

"You're going the wrong way," Brinkman cried out after him. "Anchorage is to the north."

Noah kicked in the door — felt his stomach pitch when he realized what he'd done. Zip wasn't there. It was quiet. Nothing was disturbed. Noah went to the storage room door, opened it slowly.

In the corner was Thanh, huddled under his blanket. When he saw it was Noah he stood and rushed over to him and hugged him. "Oh God, it's you!"

"You okay?"

"He was here," Thanh said.

"I know."

"I recognized his voice. He knocked on the door, called your name. I thought he was going to come in."

A calmer Noah realized a guy with Zip's criminal smarts wouldn't

105

go around breaking into offices in broad daylight. Too risky. Brinkman had seen him in the hallway and no doubt Zip saw Brinkman.

"How do you feel?" Noah asked him, gently holding him at a distance.

"All right. I'm better."

"Good, because we've got to get out of here."

It was as if it was the first time Thanh focused on Noah. "What happened?" he asked, touching Noah's face.

"Long story. Same ending. We're in deep shit, Thanh. Get dressed."

"Did Frank do that?"

"No, Hubbard isn't the only monster out there in the world."

"We need to go to the hospital."

"No," Noah said.

Thanh insisted on cleaning the cuts and abrasions, after which Noah gathered the cash and whatever stuff would help them through the next few days of uncertain habitation. The day was ahead of them.

Noah stopped in to see Brinkman.

"I'm on vacation," Noah said to the older detective, who was standing behind, and looking over the shoulder of, a new girl. No names yet, apparently.

"Convalescence is more like it. You look terrible."

"Actually I'm dead."

"In that case, you look pretty good."

"Thanks."

"But, for the record. Are you dead or on vacation?"

"Make it dead, okay?"

"Dead man walking."

"Dead man limping."

As the car crossed under the huge orange girders of the Golden Gate, Noah remembered he had to be very careful. No drivers license. No I.D. No PI license, for that matter. The sun was full now and once they were beyond the crassly commercial slice of San Rafael, the ride would be pleasant.

Thanh reached for the radio. "You mind?"

"I don't mind. But I'm afraid all you'll get is static."

He smiled and sat back.

"You want me to sing?" Noah asked. He didn't get an answer. "Are you afraid?"

"Of you singing? A little."

"No. Of Zip Hubbard?"

"Is that what you call him?"

"That's his nickname. You knew he was a killer, didn't you? I mean professionally. That's how he made his money."

Thanh's face went sad, then blank.

"Sorry," Noah said. "I'm not often let out to play among real human beings."

Thanh shook his head.

"You loved him."

"Not any more. Let's not talk about it."

"What'd you do before?"

"Before?"

"Before you met the guy we're not going to talk about."

"That seems like so long ago."

"Were you on the streets?"

"No. You mean . . . ? No." He thought for a moment, then smiled. "I guess you could say I was a showgirl." He waited for a response. "St. Louis, Chicago, Indianapolis, Cincinnati, Louisville. Midwest. I met what's his name in Chicago. He brought me out here."

"So you didn't . . . ?"

"No. Not then. I never really sold my body . . . until . . . at least not directly."

"What's that supposed to mean?"

"What it means. I had relationships with guys who could take care of me, give me a roof, food, an occasional gift. You know, just like the second wives of various successful businessmen. You know, a trophy wife. Isn't that what they say? In fact, I was the wife of various. . . ." He looked at Noah and smiled. "Same thing isn't it?"

They looked as the interstate opened up to pleasant, rolling hills and a great big sky.

"Tell me if I'm getting stupid again."

"All right."

"It's kind of personal."

"Go ahead."

"Are you going to become a woman? I mean . . . completely." Noah asked.

"No."

"No?"

"No. I'm keeping my penis."

There was quiet for a few miles before Thanh began to speak.

"I thought . . . at one time . . . maybe. But no. I'm happy. I don't mean in my present situation, but I'm happy with myself, with who I am."

After a moment of silence, Thanh continued. "When I was very young, I thought I was supposed to be a man. When I got older, I was sure I was supposed to be a woman, because being male didn't feel right. I wore my mother's clothes. I practiced flirting the way she did with the soldiers. When I came here, I decided I'd find a way to go through with it, the entire transformation. I took hormones for awhile, got these implants. A starter set." He smiled. "And then, I decided I was where I was supposed to be. I didn't want to be a woman. I didn't want to be a man. The rules are so silly for both of them."

"Silly."

"To define yourself that way. For me anyway. I'm comfortable now. Even though I may make others uncomfortable. This is me. I am happy."

"You're happy! You and two or three other people in the world. And I think they're institutionalized," Noah said.

"And you?"

"I'm keeping mine too."

"That's not what I meant," Thanh said laughing.

"How is it you know so many languages?"

"My father was Hispanic like I said. I had some time once. I decided to learn the language."

"Your father. . . ."

"A soldier. An American soldier. He told her his parents were from Chile. Anyway, he dropped by, got my mom pregnant, went home when his time was up. She said he made love in Spanish. That he cursed in Spanish. That he said goodbye in English. Thanh didn't smile. He was silent, but broke the silence later. "You know they call people who know two languages 'bilingual.' You know what they call people who only know one language?"

"Monolingual?"

"No. American." Thanh smiled. His eyes were alive again.

"You speak Spanish and Vietnamese as well as you speak English?"

"Vietnamese is my language. English, I'm getting there. But every once in a while, if I'm not careful, my accent will slip back in. I might say 'bitch' when I mean 'beach.' Want to go to the bitch?"

"No, I met her the other day and she's trying to kill me."

"Okay, my turn."

"Your turn?"

"To ask questions."

"All right."

"Okay, here's what I want to know," Thanh said. "You have to answer."

"I have to answer. All right."

"Would you do a guy for $100,000?"

"Kill? No. Of course not."

"No, not kill. Give head." Silence. "To a guy, I mean."

"The answer is 'no,'" Noah said. "What kind of question is that?"

"A question. Just a question. Don't get upset."

"I'm not upset."

"You seem upset."

There was a moment of silence.

"All right, I was upset for a minute. I'm not upset now. The answer is 'no.'"

"Okay, a million dollars?" Thanh asked.

"What?"

"A million dollars. You do him for 30 seconds. That's all."

Noah winced. The whole image of a big hairy. . . . He pushed the image out of his head. "No. The answer is 'no.' Are we done with this subject?"

"One more."

"No."

"You asked me some pretty personal questions. I answered them."

"Not about. . . ."

"About intimate things. About my life, my feelings. About maybe I'm a whore, about maybe I want to have my penis chopped off. That's not personal?"

Thanh's slow delivery of a smile won him over.

"You win. One more. Just one more if we're on this same screwy line of questioning." Not much traffic on the interstate, but Noah kept his eyes on the road.

"All right," Thanh turned his body toward Noah, concentrated on his face. "Picture someone you love more than anyone and anything in the world."

"Okay." He had his wife's picture slipping in, unwanted. But it was there. Who else was there? His mind pictured her when she was young, soon after they met. She was crying. She was afraid of loving him, she said.

"Are you picturing someone?"

"Yes, dammit."

"Now picture a gun at this person's head. It's cocked. There's a finger on the trigger. And if you don't give this guy a blowjob, he's going to blow the brains out of the person you love."

"Jesus," Noah said. "Let's not . . . this is. . . ." He hit the steering wheel with his hand and the sound reverberated. "Yes," he said. "Yes, I would. I've said it. Yes. Now what in the hell does that have to do with anything?"

"Lots of things. But it really has nothing to do with blow jobs."

Noah just kept shaking his head. What was it about Thanh that made Noah so nervous at one moment, so uncharacteristically compassionate the next, and so goddamned pissed off the moment after that. Noah was so deep in thought, he almost missed his turn.

"You're a brat, you know that?"

"A beach," Thanh said, grinning.

Noah started to say something, but the words went away, only empty breath came out. He shook his head again.

Quiet settled in. Just the hum of the engine. The day was cheery enough and the frequent glances Noah made in the rear view and side mirrors showed not one silver Porsche Boxster. Noah had gone various speeds for sustained periods of time to determine if a clever Zip was following in a rental car.

Thanh broke the silence.

"Do you like me better with short hair?" Noah gave him a look. "Well then," Thanh countered the look. "Do you like me less worse?"

"Less worse?" This time the head shaking included a grin. Why was he smiling? Perhaps he was just worn out, giving in. "Sometimes you are very frustrating."

"In a lovable sort of way." Thanh was flirting. "Call me 'Nguyen.'"

"Call you what?"

"Nguyen."

"I thought you were Thanh. And before that you were Sasha. Who are you?"

"My name is Nguyen Thanh."

"How many more names do you have?"

"I used to perform as 'Pearl.'"

"How did all of this happen? I was minding my business. . . ."

"No you weren't. That night you were out driving. You saw me . . . you know what you wanted."

"All right, let's not get into what I wanted. I'm sorry I brought it up. I didn't mean just you. I meant everything. You've got an obsessive lover. . . ."

"Ex-lover."

"Ex-lover, who is also a professional killer, a damned good one apparently, who is after both of us. And I've stirred up some nameless, faceless death squad, who probably intended that I perish and will be fucking pissed when they find out that I didn't. Now, some people win the lottery, or inherit millions from some forgotten uncle. Some people. . . some people even die in plane crashes or quickly and painlessly in their sleep or get struck by lightning. And then, Thanh, there's alien abduction, body probes. . . ."

"Hmmmnnn," Thanh smiled.

"Quiet. What are the odds? The odds are that most people will not experience anything so rare, so random as an alien abduction. Now me," Noah said, his voice beginning to trail off, "I have two — not one, but two — different and unrelated killers on my tail."

"Look at the bright side. You got a chance to meet me before you die. Or is this just another alien abduction?"

"I liked you better when you were sick. You slept and didn't ask stupid questions."

"It's a sunny day, a beautiful drive. I enjoy being with you."

Noah managed an odd smile. He wasn't sure how he felt. Intimacy with anyone was strange. People he knew now didn't say "I enjoy being with you." People didn't ask him personal questions.

This whole thing with Thanh was confusing. Was it physical? Was it mental? What did it mean to him that he still saw Thanh as something sexual? He thought he'd gotten beyond all these petty judgments. He wondered why he was still threatened. He was mad that he was still threatened. Still, he was threatened. Thanh's presence, just being there, made Noah question everything, including now his own identity.

"Isn't anyone who they say they are?" Noah asked the roof of his Alfa Romeo. "Or think they are," he almost added. Thanh dozed. The sunlight and heat coming in from the window acted as a sleeping potion. He didn't wake until they stopped at the motel outside Calistoga, the one where Noah had stayed before.

The woman at the desk couldn't keep her eyes off Thanh and it was quite clear she was having difficulty making sense of things. Thanh had to have noticed the sidelong glances, the puzzlement that showed in her expression; but he was very polite. Noah wasn't quite sure which image was more puzzling to strangers. A boy in a dress or a woman with a flat top? And in fact, Thanh was neither. Or both.

As Noah aged, the universe made continually less sense.

"I'll be back in a few hours," Noah said warding off any questions from Thanh about going with him. "We'll find something to eat when I get back. I know a great restaurant up here. We'll find a way to enjoy the evening."

FIFTEEN

THE SUN GLISTENED off Morcham's aluminum trailer. Noah approached it with more than a little trepidation. He had been warned. His first line would be "Rawley is dead." He'd rehearsed that simple line as if he were a character in a play: "The king is dead." Perhaps the suddenness of such a dramatic revelation would at least disarm the man emotionally and they could move on to more important issues — such as "who did it?" If it weren't for the silly old notion that the Rawley murderers wanted to eliminate Noah as well, he wouldn't be risking his life. If that weren't the case, there would be little to gain. Certainly the idea of compensation no longer applied. And curiosity wasn't motive enough to stand in front of an angry, unstable personality holding a gun.

When he saw Morcham at the door, pistol shining in concert with the trailer and the writer's menacing metal prosthesis, Noah wished he'd made a different choice. He wished it were Brinkman's gun weighing down his right coat pocket rather than Olympia's cell phone.

"Charles Rawley is dead," Noah said on cue. Morcham's face froze and he failed to raise the pistol that was in his good hand. Noah nodded, a sort of self-congratulation, a desperately needed pat on the back, worthwhile even if it was his own hand doing the patting. His ego needed a few strokes.

From stone, Morcham's face reanimated. "I don't believe it."

"I was there."

"So you say."

"Watch the news?" Noah asked. Morcham didn't answer. "The explosion near China Basin in San Francisco."

"Fireworks," Morcham said.

"What?"

"Fireworks. They called in the feds. Illegal fireworks." He looked at Noah's face as if he were going to be able to cipher something. "They brought the firearms and tobacco people. Somebody was storing fireworks and. . . ."

"No. I was there. A helicopter fired a missile."

Morcham was quiet. His blinks and lack of hostility suggested that his bitter brain was considering the possibility.

"Charles Rawley," Noah continued, "was in the back of a semi trailer with some goons in dark suits in the middle of the night. I was supposed to be contacting his kidnappers at the request of his wife, Olympia. Only that's not how it really is."

"How is it really?" Morcham asked, looking down at Noah from the top step, pistol still to his side.

"Rawley wasn't kidnapped. I wasn't what they expected. They thought I was bringing papers for some sort of merger or something. I thought all I was supposed to be was an intermediary with the kidnappers."

"Only there were no kidnappers?"

"No. Rawley was there willingly. He was in charge. I was kidnapped. Rawley phoned someone named 'Nora.'"

Morcham's eyes widened. "Come in," he said in a tone that was nearly friendly.

Apparently, the secret word was "Nora."

Inside was so crowded it seemed impossible for one to inhabit the space in any practical way. Stacks of books, papers, magazines and newspapers allowed the narrowest of pathways. Only the stovetop and a narrow bed were spared the litter. Morcham motioned for Noah to sit on the bed, while Morcham himself went to the desk, sat on a folding chair, and fingered the laptop computer, using one hand's digits to type in something before closing the lid.

"You know this Nora?" Morcham asked.

"I don't know if I know this Nora or not. Do you?"

"We're going to have a little power struggle here, I think."

"Look, someone put me in harm's way with the specific intent that I be harmed. Out of existence. I don't like that."

Morcham smiled. At least Noah interpreted the twist in the man's lips as a smile. He found Noah's statement humorous in a bitter, arrogant sort of way. With what the writer might have had to go through, Noah could easily forgive him the attitude. After all, weren't they on the same side?

Noah continued: "Who would want to kill Charles Rawley?"

"Any number of people," Morcham said.

"And who would have the resources to do it by missile."

"Is that what you think happened?"

"I don't think it, Mr. Morcham. I know it."

"And just how did you manage to outrun a missile?"

"I heard it . . . a premonition, maybe."

"A premonition."

"I was in the military, the Navy. I did a lot of helicopter training. I recognized the sound."

"Yeah, well. . . ."

"Rawley was traveling with some hired goons. Black suits, unmarked cars. Real professional."

"Hayden Security. Private investigation and protection. International. Rawley owns them."

"Owned them. Looks to me like they didn't do their job. So, who's behind the assassination and why?"

"Probably a coup."

"You breathing a little easier, Mr. Morcham?" Noah asked, surprised that the news of Rawley's death didn't make more of an impression.

"A little. You on the run, are you?" Morcham's eyebrows raised as a mark to the question. Noah wasn't sure he could recognize madness from a facial expression, but Morcham's look sure looked like madness to him.

"I'm not sure they know I'm even alive."

Another sardonic smile and an expression that could have been inspired by an acid bath. Noah's thoughts went to Rawley. How much harm must he have done to this man to twist him so severely.

"Back to Nora. You know her?"

"Probably," Noah said. "The woman who hired me. Said her name was 'Olympia.' I think I've been made a fool of, in a very large way."

"Hmmmnnn," Morcham said, nodding agreement or approval. "Yes, you have. You most certainly have." Morcham, raised the pistol, aiming it between Noah's eyes. "Stay seated Mr. Private Eye. Don't make any sudden moves. I need to find out what to do with you."

Morcham's eyes traveled over Noah's body. "Carefully now, very deliberately, empty your pockets."

Noah did as he was told, but there wasn't much to empty. No wallet. Just car keys, a pair of sunglasses, Olympia's cell phone, two dimes and some $100 bills.

"You don't have much."

"No. My wallet was blown up."

"I see. You always carry your phone?"

"It's Olympia's."

"Oh?"

"I was to call her once I identified Mr. Rawley."

"Really. You know her number?" He seemed happily surprised.

"No."

"No?" Morcham laughed. "You had a phone to call her, but you didn't have her number. You're not cooperating."

"Look, Morcham. . . ."

"My sense is that your death was not only expected, but planned, so if I can't locate Nora in a few moments, I'm sure no one will mind if I kill you."

"It's programmed to call her," Noah said to buy some time.

"Hmmmnn." Morcham pondered the information.

"You don't have her number?" Noah asked, aware now that Morcham was no doubt part of the same operation that eliminated Rawley. And that he had — continuing the grand march of his stupidity — marched right into the Briar Patch.

"In the interests of anonymity, phone records being so easily accessible, perhaps I could use your phone." Noah wasn't about to engage in any power games with Morcham. He reached down, picked up the phone. "Push the appropriate code and hand it to me."

Noah keyed in the pound sign and the nine key three times. He heard the ring and handed it to Morcham, whose metal pincers clutched the phone. He brought the phone to his ear and in a moment began to speak . . . "Nor. . . ."

Suddenly Morcham's eyes widened in surprise or horror or both — phone and gun fell to the floor and he fell limply, face first onto his desk.

Noah backed away quickly toward the door. He had seen, or thought he saw, a fine spray, barely a mist, come from the receiver of the phone. Noah was out the door, stumbling back off the steps, falling on the dusty ground.

A gas. Rigged. It was meant to kill Noah. A failsafe device activated if something had gone terribly wrong or if Noah waited until he was away from the targeted Rawley when he made the call to Olympia . . . or Nora. Or?

Noah left the trailer door open. Because Noah was not killed by the same poison that gave Morcham his last breath — despite his proximity to the victim — it was likely death came from a highly concentrated dose of vapor now dispersed. The same dismal luck that had put Noah in jeopardy had now worked for him — sort of. How many times had he been ready to dial that coded number and talk to Olympia? And now, this booby-trapped cell phone may have saved his life.

Getting up from the ground he thought for a moment about calling the police. Leaving the scene of a crime is just the kind of thing that trips people up. The little details. Perhaps it wasn't wise to call them after all, he decided. Noah had no I.D. and couldn't provide a convincing argument for being there. Worse, telling the Calistoga or the Napa County police about Morcham's gaseous, James Bondian death, not to mention explaining corporate storm troopers with missile firing helicopters who wanted him dead would make Noah a candidate for the local psycho ward.

"Careful now officer, my finger actually shoots a death ray. All I have to do is hold my breath, close my eyes and think of Don Knotts."

As far as Noah could figure, Morcham wasn't the type to have many guests. No telling how long it would take before the body was discovered. Did it matter? Did anything matter? Who would believe Noah? Who would support him? Why, he had the perfect supporter, didn't he? An illegal immigrant, an on-the-run transvestite who was once the "house boy" of a hit man.

He walked out to his car and drove back to the motel.

There would be fingerprints on the phone, Noah thought. But at the moment, he wasn't sure he cared.

Thanh enjoyed the restaurant and enjoyed recounting his previous adventures in wine country restaurants. The French Laundry in Yountville. Bistro Ralph in Healdsburg. Noah dismissed any notion of budgeting for the moment and found that Thanh knew his way around the wine list, or seemed to. It wouldn't take much to fool Noah.

Despite Noah's recent proximity to death — Morcham's and his own nearly — he was able to relax and enjoyed the conversation with Thanh, who was determined to keep it light. Movies. Books. Noah could see Zip Hubbard and Sasha as an attractive, engaging couple in fine restaurants and exclusive clubs. That was all over with for Thanh. He was back to zero. And after dinner, this little fantasy would be over as well.

A long, hard look at the immediate future would have to take place tonight. They didn't have the money to continue to stay in motels indefinitely, no matter how frugal they were. On the other hand, returning home would likely get them killed. Thanh was in the most danger. It might be days before the group that killed Rawley — Olympia and Company — would discover that Noah was still alive. On the third hand, Hubbard likely knew Thanh was alive and wasn't too happy about it. How he knew was another question. Had Rose or Stern tipped him off?

"You know," Noah said to Thanh when they returned to their room at the motel. "It might be smart if we get you upstate or maybe to Portland."

Thanh didn't say anything. He didn't even look up from the newspaper.

"Portland's big enough to get lost in for awhile, yet it's not a place where Hubbard is likely to have connections."

"I don't know," Thanh said, voice weak. Then stronger. "It might be a good idea."

"Yeah, it might be. A name change. That sort of thing. Maybe Canada. Vancouver is nice, they say."

His suggestion hung in the air like stale smoke.

"Thanh, I'm trying to think this through. We have serious problems here. Both of us."

"I know."

"You're a good kid," he said to Thanh, who didn't reply. Noah didn't wonder why. The statement was hollow. Insincere. Worse, condescending. He wished he hadn't said it. "That's stupid. A stupid thing to say. I'm sorry."

"Don't worry about it," Thanh said flatly. He nodded toward the television. He got up, went to the bathroom and closed the door.

Noah used the remote to increase the volume.

". . . . police are saying that the explosion near Central Basin last night was a result of a stockpile of illegal fireworks. Saying that the incident was part of a larger investigation, authority has been turned over to the federal government. However, what we have learned since this morning is that officials at the U.S. Bureau of Alcohol, Firearms and Tobacco have admitted there is evidence of some fatalities."

Noah could hear the water running through the louvered door.

". . . . there are no witnesses to the explosion that happened in the early morning hours on a remote stretch of bay land scheduled for redevelopment. . . ."

Noah shook his head. Morcham was right. What happened there had been covered up. The government was involved. But how far? Were they just trying to keep the facts undercover in order to make their investigation more effective? Or were they part of the operation that eliminated Rawley as a powerful player on the international scene?

All of it was beyond Noah.

The door opened. Thanh came out, fresh faced. "I can sleep on the floor," he said.

"No, no, I will. I'm used to less than luxurious accommodations. A pillow. . . ." It all seemed so silly all of a sudden. "Hey, it's a big bed."

"Fuckin' right," Thanh said, voice dropping a few octaves.

"Yeah," Noah said smiling. "Fuckin' A." It was all so funny, so mixed up. Deep voice, baby face, butch hair, breasts.

Thanh grinned.

The bed was queen-sized. Thanh was on one side, at the edge, body turned away. It was if he was trying to make himself smaller, perhaps invisible.

"Why did you stay with him so long?" Noah's voice seemed loud after the moments of dark silence.

119

Noah heard the rustling of sheets as Thanh turned.

"He wasn't what you think. It was wonderful at first. I was in love. He was too. We talked, about our past, about our dreams. We listened to music. We would go out to dinner — the most wonderful food . . . and wine . . . and conversation. I would dress for him. Not cheap. Not gaudy, but subtle, sophisticated. I fooled them and Frank would beam. All those men in the restaurant jealous of him, jealous of Frank and me. They didn't know."

Thanh laughed.

"I was special in his eyes," Thanh said.

"What happened?"

"I don't know. It went to hell little by little. He'd stay away longer and longer. We would go out less and less. He'd become more moody, then violent, then more violent." After a moment or two, Thanh said. "He had his demons. I guess he couldn't keep them at bay any longer."

"I'm sorry. I wanted to know why you waited, why you left when you did?"

"He was going to kill me, Noah. What else is there to say? Please, let's sleep. I don't want to go back to that place in my life."

"Good night," Noah said. "Sweet dreams." He meant it.

Another century of quiet.

"I do worry, Thanh."

"Don't," he said, without turning back. "I'm not as fragile as you think."

Thanh was a riddle. A Sasha. A Thanh. The Sphinx, Noah thought, or some other great mystery. A lion's body and the head and breasts of a woman.

Uneasy with his own thoughts, Noah tried to block them. He couldn't. He was drawn to Nuygen Thanh. Drawn to what? What part? Strangely, it wasn't only Thanh's beauty and grace that caused confusion, it was because Noah was beginning to realize that Thanh was becoming real to him. For years, Noah was content to see the rest of humanity as separate capsules floating in the same space.

This was no longer the case with Thanh. There were dimensions. Too many dimensions. It was as if each of their souls were leaking into each other. And even if he could bring himself to admit the sexual attraction, physical intimacy with Thanh now would not be a harmless act of gratification. It could not be rationalized away as an indiscretion that had to do with too much alcohol, too much testosterone.

It was a long time before Noah could sleep. He could hear the building settle, the rise and fall of the wind, the eventual easy rhythms of Thanh's sleeping breaths. The temptation had passed. Noah would not wake him.

Noah must have fallen asleep eventually, because he woke to the sounds of movement in the light filled room. It was Thanh. He was up, dressed and busy gathering what few belongings he had brought with him.

"You're up?"

"Did I wake you?"

Noah thought he looked so serious.

"No. What are you doing?"

"I'm leaving."

There was a kindly distance in his tone.

"It'll take me a few minutes. . . ." Noah started to say, getting out of bed.

"No. Just me."

"Let's have breakfast and. . . ."

"Go look in the bathroom."

Noah, carrying the last vestiges of sleep with him, stumbled toward the bath. There, on the mirror, was a message scrawled in lipstick.

> *Nu, sweetheart A lovely couple*
> *Guess where you're going*
> *on your honeymoon*

SIXTEEN

THERE WAS DOUBT, of course. Unwanted suspicion wormed its way into his mind. What if . . . just what if Thanh had written the message? He was staring at the reddish block letters that seemed imprinted on his own face as he looked into the bathroom mirror. Why? Why would Thanh do this? To dramatize his dilemma? Get sympathy? It didn't make sense; but little made sense.

How could Hubbard have gotten through a locked and double-bolted door? Was he asked to believe that Hubbard came in, fiddled around in the bathroom and left without anyone being aware of it? If Zip Hubbard could do that, why wouldn't he have just taken them out? A couple of quiet bullets into their skulls would have remedied Hubbard's anger or obsession or whatever it was. All that risk for what? A joke? This was incredible.

Noah had never been one to trust others — not for years now. But never before was deceit so rampant in his life, never before had it played such a disturbing role in every moment of his existence. It was clear though, once he thought about it. Of course Hubbard could have gotten in and out undetected. He's a professional killer, for Christ's sake. And playing this little joke was very much part of his nature. Hadn't Noah witnessed Hubbard's cold, sadistic nature first hand? This, in fact, was just like him. Torment the helpless victims before doing them in. Make them squirm, feel his power.

The dilemma was that no matter what Noah believed these days, it was usually wrong. He came back into the room as Thanh was putting his change back into his pockets.

"We'll do better if we stick together," Noah said.

"He wants *me*." Thanh said this clearly. He'd made his decision. There were no doubts.

"Maybe. Maybe not."

"I can slip away easier if I'm by myself." Again, it was clear Thanh was serious, but anger or defiance began to creep into his face, his tone. He locked his jaw when he stopped speaking.

"You came to me. . . ."

"This isn't your problem," Thanh said with uncharacteristic harshness. Then he softened. "I appreciate what you've done. You're a wonderful man. . . ." He stopped. Noah was sure Thanh stopped to shut out the emotion that began to inhabit his voice. "I thought . . . and I had no right to think . . ." His chin quivered. "Fuck, damn, shit," he said. He bolted toward the door.

"No!" Noah went to the door, pushed it shut, falling against it and nearly crushing Thanh's delicate body. He was face to face with Thanh. Eye to eye. Breath to breath. Very close. Too close.

Noah didn't know what he was feeling. It was foreign, frightening.

"Noah," Thanh said steadily, voice controlled so much it was monotone. "I have go . . . now . . . by myself."

"Do you really want to?" Noah still held him there, pressed against the door.

"No."

"Then?"

"Then? I think . . . I'm falling in love with you," Thanh said. "That's an impossible thing, isn't it?"

"Isn't it always?" Noah backed away. "Stay. I'm not backing out of this now." He knew that he had just backed out of a critical moment, a telling moment.

Noah turned and went to the bed. He sat on the edge.

Though he managed to stay standing, Thanh's body went limp, as if someone had just knocked all the air from his lungs. He took a couple of deep breaths and moved toward Noah.

Thanh looked at Noah soberly. "Can you beat him?"

"If I'm lucky, maybe."

Thanh shook his head. "I'm very selfish Noah. I can't bear the idea I caused your death."

"He's going to get us both, Thanh. Both of us. We don't stand a chance hopping away like little rabbits in the woods."

"Why would I want to meet with my former house boy?" Zip showed calm, amusement, as his raspy voice entered Noah's office over the speaker phone.

"I have something you want," Thanh said.

"Do you really?"

"And I want to return it to you, personally."

"Something of mine? Maybe the watch you lifted?"

Thanh's lips pressed together and his eyes hardened.

"I don't steal. You know that."

"Look young man, I'm sorry your years of service to me ended the way it did. Your friends. Your drug habit. I tried to help, but you weren't trying. I wish you well in all your future endeavors."

"I'm not taping this conversation, Frank."

"I didn't say you were."

"I want closure. I want to see you face to face. I want to tell you goodbye."

"Well, goodbye. Goodbye Nu. See ya around the pool."

"I want to work this out. I know you can find me wherever I am. But I have a little insurance. I'm not a fool."

"I'll be the judge of that."

"Judge this," Thanh said with force. "I have enough on you to put you away. Anything happens to me, I go with the knowledge that you won't be very far behind. I will be there waiting by the pool, Frank."

Noah was surprised at Thanh's toughness.

"What is this . . . ahhhh . . . policy you have?" Zip kept a skeptical, bemused tone in his voice.

"I'll show you. I'll show you half of it. I want to meet."

"Come on over."

"No," Thanh said. "I'm setting the place. I'm setting the time. And I'm setting the conditions."

Zip's laughter sounded real. Thanh shook his head, put his hand over the phone and took a deep breath.

"Okay, kid," Zip said. The "kid" part hit Noah in the stomach. Thanh didn't flinch.

"Rigoletto's."

"The coffee shop on Columbus?"

"Yes. Outside."

"Why outside?"

"I want to be in public, and able to make a quick exit," Thanh said. Zip laughed. "At ten in the morning."

"You got it, kid. Ten o'clock."

"Don't be late. I'm not going to sit there waiting for you and end up a target," Thanh said.

"All right."

"Frank?"

"What?"

"I want you to do me one favor."

"What's that?"

"Wear the scarf I gave you. That blue one."

"The purple faggot scarf?"

"Yeah. That one."

"What in the hell for?"

"Call it a good faith gesture."

"If I don't?"

"I won't be there. I loved you, Frank. I'm doing this because of that. I'm trying to negotiate a way out of trouble for both of us. I want you to wear the scarf and think of me, think of what we had . . . and. . . ." Thanh took a breath. His face didn't match the warmth in his voice. ". . . and . . . what we could have."

"You think you can really hurt me, Nu?"

"No, no. You can really hurt me. You already have. Death might even be a favor. But hurt you? I'm not sure anything hurts you. I doubt if even your dying would hurt you. This one favor, Frank. If what I've got is nothing, you've lost nothing. You can say goodbye in person instead of scribbling a note on the mirror."

"I have no idea what you're talking about. But you've got me curious. If just spending a few moments with you will get you off my back, then let's do it. Oh . . . Nu . . . you're handling yourself pretty well. I'm proud of you. You were damned near a match for me. You know that? Almost.

125

But you have a little too much heart. That'll do you in every time."

"You'll wear the scarf?"

"I'll wear it like a flag, kiddo."

Dial tone.

They went out to the Richmond, Clement Street for Chinese. Noah didn't know what to say. The decision, which seemed to be the only one he could make, now weighed heavily upon him. He hadn't fully shared everything with Thanh. "Trust me," Noah said, when Thanh wanted to know what they were doing. For Noah, it was important they not have this conversation.

"How did you get to the states?" Noah asked to move the conversation away from Zip.

"Long story," Thanh said.

Noah started to say that they had all night. They did. But Thanh's declaration of love, and the awkward moment that followed, put a strain on spontaneity.

"I'm sorry," Noah said, waiting until the waiter brought the big bowl of sweet and sour soup. "If you don't want to talk. . . ." He didn't wait to finish his sentence or for Thanh to respond. "Be right back. Wash my hands."

In the hallway, he telephoned Brinkman. Brinkman was reluctant at first — not wanting to use his connections — but Noah promised him a modest fee. Next, Noah called the number he had memorized.

"Olympia?"

"What a surprise, Noah."

"I'm sure it is. I'm speaking to you from the third rung of hell and reversing the charges. And you know, everything is long distance from down here."

"I'm glad you called. You don't know how worried. . . ."

"I want my money," Noah said. He was pretty sure he was never going to get it, but he wanted her to think that greed was his motive for calling. "I want to arrange a meeting."

When Noah came back to the table, Thanh looked up. "Boat."

"Boat?"

"When I was eleven my mother put me on a boat. She said something

126

about the Communists. I don't know anything about that, about why the communists would have wanted me. That's what I remember."

Noah nodded. Vietnam was pretty much history by the time Noah joined the Navy. But he knew what happened when the U.S. finally decided to bow out. Friends, lovers, children were left behind. Some, in desperation, boarded rickety boats and set out on a dangerous voyage. No one knows just how many were lost at sea. And even the boats that finally made it to some shore, the travelers, those who had not succumbed to disease or starvation, those strong ones who survived were put into camps, virtual prisons.

"Galang Camp. Indonesia. I was there two years. I wasn't going to get out. I had no money to bribe the authorities. And I wasn't a woman. I had nothing to bargain with then." Thanh looked at Noah. He went on. "One day a water tower fell. On three of us. One was killed — a woman. Another man's leg was injured seriously. I suffered a concussion. This man and I were taken to some place, a clinic or something. If it was a hospital, it wasn't like hospitals here or in Saigon. The man died. I left."

"You left, just like that?"

"They kept me overnight. I think they thought I was too weak or too out of it to go anywhere. They were wrong." He took a bite of his food.

No doubt Thanh left out volumes. These weren't scout camps. However, he wasn't telling the story to get comfort, just to answer the question.

Thanh stopped to sip his tea and to eat. Noah noticed how Thanh raised his rice bowl as he used the chopsticks to shovel the rice into his mouth as one learns to do when rice is eaten daily. Perhaps it was the trip back in time and place.

"We don't have to talk about this if you don't want to," Noah said, thinking that any conversation, including this one, was better than relating the telephone conversations Noah had conducted in the hall.

"There was no place to go. And I was captured. I was brought in for discipline and in the office was an American. I remember how he looked at me. Maybe it was instinct, I'm not sure. But in two weeks I was on a boat to Tanjumg Pinang and then to Singapore, where the man I had seen in the office was waiting for me."

The waiter came by to ask if they needed anything. Noah needed another beer to cool his palate from the heat of the Chinese peppers, a piece of which he must have actually ingested.

"He liked young boys," Thanh said when the waiter departed. "His friends liked young boys. I don't know exactly what he did for a living. He didn't talk about it, but when he went back to America, I came with him."

"Did you like him?"

"I didn't hate him. Affection didn't enter into it, I guess. He wasn't a bad man exactly. He didn't abuse me, but he wasn't someone I could love. He didn't love me either, just loved . . . ," his voice trailed off. "He would bring them home, want me to do things . . ." Thanh shook his head. "Soon, it was clear I had become too old for him or too familiar. I couldn't go to school because I had no papers. I couldn't apply for work for fear they would ask too many questions. He didn't want me being out on the streets. He didn't want the neighbors to see me. Except for television and books, it was becoming like being in Galang Camp. When I tried to look at my future, I couldn't see one."

"How did he get you into this country?"

"I don't know. It was long ago. I had some sort of temporary papers. The American had arranged things. He was high up in the government somewhere. Maybe Foreign Service, I'm not sure. That's why I couldn't go out, he told me. They would find out I was an alien and ship me back to Vietnam or the Camp and he would be in a lot of trouble. He saved my life, he said, when I told him how unhappy I was. I asked him 'for what?' And he didn't know."

"And then you left?"

"He wanted me to go live with this other man. I knew the one. I couldn't."

The beer came and it ended the conversation. The two of them ate quietly, Noah wondering if he could have survived being used and tossed around the way Thanh had been, still was.

"He didn't kill me though," Thanh said. "When he was tired of me, he didn't try to kill me."

Another restless night's sleep for Noah. He longed for the earlier days, not so long ago, when his emotions were anesthetized by a few bottles of beer, when right and wrong played no part in his daily activities, when he had no responsibilities real or imagined, when his life wasn't on the verge of being snuffed out, when he didn't engage in such silly questions as who he was, who he really was.

What was worse was that he was chastised by the example of Thanh's life. Noah had no such hardships to overcome. His own life had been, by comparison, relatively easy, devoid of any real challenges. Aside from Sarah, and the events surrounding their separation, Noah lived a blessed life, one full of opportunities, and yet he'd done nothing but drift. What could he have done if he had Thanh's strength, Thanh's will? Thanh's courage?

How strange . . . how tenuous is our place in the universe, he thought. A random event changes everything. Thanh on a street corner. Olympia finding his office. His life is changed. Random. Random. Certainly love was random. At the moment, he wanted to be with Thanh, feeling the warmth of his body. Is that all he wanted?

He knew he would not make the move. But would he push Thanh away if. . . . ?

SEVENTEEN

Morning visited Noah. Thanh hadn't. Noah was thankful he hadn't been put to a test. The intrusion of daylight helped reshape his thoughts. Perhaps it was the gravity of the day's events that caused him to think so soberly.

The clock radio said eight. They had two hours to North Beach. He knocked on the storage room door and opened it, catching Thanh while he dressed. Thanh held his shirt up to hide his chest.

"I'm up," Thanh said.

"Okay." Noah quietly closed the door and went to the bathroom, washing his face. He thought about shaving, decided not to. Grungy was appropriate. He put coffee on. There was something about the day, about the reality of the day. Everything seemed clear, absolutely clear. He was completely aware of every movement he made as he fixed the coffee.

It was as if somehow perception was heightened. He was focused. Everything had been prioritized. When Thanh came from the back room, dressed now, Noah saw him in a more defined way. Last night he had realized Thanh was a person who'd gone through hell and maintained his own personal dignity. Thanh, if uncomfortable in an unkind and unwelcoming world, was comfortable in himself, in his own skin. There was something noble in that and in his beauty.

Did Thanh know how the morning would unfold? Noah hadn't told him. For a number of reasons. He didn't want Thanh to be complicit. He didn't want him to suddenly do something foolish when the plan became real. Maybe, because Thanh never knew what the future held, he had grown accustomed to uncertainty. Maybe he preferred it. Whatever it was, he didn't ask questions.

The morning, like Noah's state of mind, was cool and crisp. The sun was out, but had not yet warmed the air. It was exhilarating. Noah thought he ought to be frightened, but he wasn't.

They walked to Market beyond Powell, where they passed the usual market place circus. Hundreds of tourists had already lined up to board the cable cars and there was the standard preacher with a sandwich board and an electronic megaphone, spewing sentences from the Bible, and adding his own flavor of doom to adulterers and sodomites. Then to Stockton. With parking impossible in North Beach and with time on their hands, walking seemed the best option. But there were other reasons to walk as well.

"What should I tell them?" Thanh asked.

"Who you are," Noah said. "The police just need to verify that you are alive. They know the body they found in the ruins isn't you. But they want to see you. Live and in the flesh. Tell them why you weren't in the apartment and who burned in the fire. They may already know. But confirm it for them."

Walking through the long, low tunnel between the City's busy retail district and Chinatown struck Noah not only as the passing between one culture and another, but also between thought and action, between familiar territory and the future. In a few minutes, nothing would ever be the same.

Noah chose the route through Chinatown on purpose. Though it didn't matter, he was puzzled that Thanh seemed to take so little notice of the mass of Asians on the narrow sidewalks. Live fish and turtles and frogs waiting to be selected for some family's boiling pot in the kitchen. Fruits and vegetables that Noah couldn't identify were stacked in brown boxes with Chinese pictograms above them.

The two of them walked, dodging pedestrians who gathered and brought traffic to a standstill, out into the street where men unloaded huge bags of rice and live chickens from a truck double-parked on the busy streets, already stalled with more buses and cars than they could handle.

At last they reached Broadway. The plan depended upon others, upon his predictions of their behavior, but even more on their punctuality. A

131

timely convergence of all players was necessary. From time to time he glanced about to see if Zip was tailing them. Caucasians stood out in the crowd of shoppers on this very Chinese street. No sign of Zip.

Though he wondered why Thanh was quiet, Noah was glad it was so. Perhaps Thanh would object if he knew. Maybe he did know. No matter. There was no stopping what Noah had put in motion. At the three-way intersection of Grant, Broadway and Columbus where again cultures converged, perhaps clashed, Noah guided them to the East side of Columbus. Chinatown was behind them now. The strip joints were to one side and up Columbus were a number of restaurants and coffee shops, including Rigoletto's. Noah and Thanh would walk up the other side where they would find, if all went as planned, Stern and Rose.

Noah possessed the kind of clear-headedness that he had when things were dicey, when he was repo'ing a car in the middle of the night or taking a bail jumper out of a bar in the Bayview district. His wits were about him.

The purple scarf was visible half a block away. Zip Hubbard had taken a seat outside, as he had been instructed and was facing the other direction. Doubtful he'd notice Noah and Thanh across the street from Rigoletto's. Noah plucked the pair of small binoculars from his jacket to get a closer look. No tricks. He wanted to be absolutely sure it was Hubbard. It was. He was sipping coffee and reading a book, at leisure, as if he were on vacation. As if he didn't have a care in the world. Thanh and Noah stopped in front of a store selling pottery and porcelains.

"Can I help you?" came the voice.

Noah turned to find Stern and Rose.

"Just browsing."

"Me too," Stern said. "I was looking for something Asian, maybe in prostitute. Something versatile."

"You the vic?" Rose asked Thanh.

"Intended."

"Well, you look fine," Stern chimed in. "Don't you think so, Rose?"

"Looks alive, if not lively."

"I wanted a second opinion, that's all," Stern said, pulling some papers out of his raincoat pocket. He looked at the laminated card, then back to Thanh, then to the I.D., then back, paying particular attention to Thanh's short hair.

"So you trying to be a dyke now?"

Thanh didn't answer. He showed them nothing.

"You can be just about anything you want, can't you, kid?"

"I'm very fortunate," Thanh said.

Rose laughed.

"Is that what you call it?" Stern asked, unkindness evident in the tone.

"That's what I'd call it too," Rose said. "Sort of like a Swiss Army knife, nothing this kid can't do. You got to admit that."

"I got to admit that?" Stern asked.

"Yeah. Section 8 of the penal code."

"I'll give you a penal code," Stern said, before turning to Thanh. "Speaking of penal codes, Missy . . . what's the story?"

"Stern, pretend you're human for a few minutes," Noah said.

From then on, he only heard sounds, pieces of recognizable words. His eyes were on the street. It wasn't that he recognized the car, but that he recognized the kind of car — a bland, gray-blue sedan of recent but undetermined vintage.

Thanh was telling the cops about his friend. Stern was spitting out short, combative questions.

The car slowed, but didn't stop. Noah heard nothing. He didn't have to. He knew it was over and as the car cleared the spot where Hubbard had been sitting, Hubbard could not be seen. People stood, mouths open wide. Silent, in shock. Then sound. Suddenly there was noise. Shouts. Cries. Arms flailed in the air. Bodies moved, huddled, ran.

The commotion distracted Stern and Rose.

"Call the police!" Someone yelled.

"911. Help. Someone get 911."

"For God's sake . . . someone's been shot."

Stern and Rose raced across the street, guns drawn, their London Fog raincoats flailing back behind them like capes.

Noah sighed. He was right. They took the bait. He could count on Olympia to try to kill him. She wouldn't have been in the car, of course. It would be a day probably, at least tomorrow morning, before she and her compatriots would know they got the wrong guy.

He turned back to Thanh. Thanh was still as a stone. His eyes were open and wide. He looked confused. Unbelieving. Betrayed.

"What did you think?" Noah asked him. He knew what Thanh thought. That he'd be there to talk to the police and then to finger Frank Hubbard for the murder. And Hubbard would be there for them, right across the street.

But that wouldn't have been enough. Noah knew that. Couldn't Thanh have figured that out?

After a long silence, Thanh just shook his head.

"He was trying to kill you!"

The sound of sirens filled the air.

Thanh turned, walked up Columbus at an angry pace. Noah called out after him, but Thanh just waved his arm behind him, palm out. It said "stay away" as clearly as could be said in any language.

"Nguyen!"

It had all happened quickly. It had happened exactly as Noah intended, except for Thanh. Except for Thanh's leaving.

Noah had killed his first living being. No way around it. How did he feel? Numb. He turned to look up the street. Seeing the thin figure of Thanh diminishing, Noah had a stranded in the universe kind of feeling. There was nothing. Really, there was nothing.

After some innocuous, but insinuating questions from Stern and Rose, Noah was free to go. Free to go where was a question he couldn't answer. Back to his office to wait for someone to drop by and kill him? Eventually, he suspected, he would do just that. Maybe sleep in the storage room with Brinkman's gun under his pillow. He still had no wallet, no I.D., no credit cards — just a few dollars left from the advance he got for dying on cue. Will they want their money back?

He tried to convince himself that setting up Zip was the right thing to do. It seemed right. Nearly so, anyway. Thanh was free. His stalker was eliminated. Now Nguyen Thanh was on his way to a new life. Now the source of Noah's tortuous confusion was gone. Noah tried to convince himself he was happy about that. But he wasn't.

Noah wondered if there was a moment when Hubbard knew he had been set up, that he was about to be killed. Noah hoped so. At least a second. He looked around. Zip Hubbard's body, in a black bag, was being loaded into the back of an ambulance. Some bystanders were dispersing. Others remained, talking — strangers to each other, no doubt — with an intimacy provided by a shared horror.

They would never know the story of this event. Who the man was. Why it happened. Just as they would never know about Charles Rawley and the new corporate dominions, warring behind the scenes for a sovereignty that has nothing to do with geographical borders, but everything to do with their lives and the lives of their children. This was an event in their lives — little more than a traffic accident. Its vivid terror would diminish in time or be replaced by something else — perhaps children shooting each other in some suburban school. The bombing of a city half way around the globe.

Noah searched for some desire to fill the blank spaces his mind tripped over. He had no job to think about. It was almost noon, but he wasn't hungry. The events exhausted him, but he wasn't sleepy. A drink? Yes. He could do with a drink. Two maybe. Not more than three. After all, a modicum of alertness was important now. He was still prey. Someone would have to pay for what just happened. And for what happened to Morcham and everyone in that truck trailer. And Noah was pretty sure he'd get stuck for the bill.

He went to a movie, but couldn't follow it. His mind wandered again and again to Thanh, trying to understand why Thanh was so shocked, why he would leave. Noah tried to understand himself. Why he cared why. He grabbed a beer at an Irish Bar down in the Financial District. A heavy Guinness under his belt, Noah headed back to his neighborhood hangout to finish his drinking in not necessarily friendly, but familiar surroundings. Night came early for him. About eight. He went back to his office, surprised that he was surprised that Thanh was not there.

There were two hang-ups on his message machine. Who? Thanh? Olympia? The police? The Caller I.D. reported an "out of area" message.

Noah laughed. How similar those two were in a way. They both threatened him — Olympia with death, Thanh with life. Both were damned dangerous.

He'd sleep in the storage room. No windows and only one door. Noah hoped to God that the next assassin wouldn't light the building on fire. There were no windows in the storage room. He took the pistol to bed with him. Despite four or five beers, despite his exhaustion, sleep wouldn't take him. And when he finally drifted, sinking into a twilight sleep, he nonetheless bobbed to the surface too often. Sounds, ever so slight, brought him to consciousness. Fear and hope attached itself to the sounds of car doors slamming, a shout from the street, muffled by the thick walls of the stone building and the rattle of the radiator. Fear that it was someone coming to kill him. Hope that it was Thanh coming back, forgiving him. Somehow, he was more comfortable thinking about someone trying to kill him.

Life was more unsettled than ever.

As far as Noah knew, it was still night when the phone rang.

"Get out of there," the voice said. It was Olympia's voice, strained and urgent. It took him a moment to recognize it.

"Sure, the moment I step out, some sniper blows my brains away. Though the thought is increasingly appealing, I'll pass on your kind invitation."

"Don't argue. Just get out and get out quick."

"Advice from my best friend."

"I have no time to explain. If you want to save your ass, get the fuck out of there." Her voice was stronger. Anger was creeping in.

"I bet you can't see me shaking my head in disbelief? Then again, maybe you can."

"I may need you. I will need you."

"For what?"

"Protection."

"Sorry. Based on my employment record with your firm, I'm giving my two-second notice."

"You'll need me."

"Like another missile up my butt."

"If I go public with what I know, I need a witness. Otherwise I'll just sound like some crazy woman upset that her husband has been killed. No one will take me seriously."

"Hey, I got an idea. Let's talk about you for awhile."

"You too. What's your life worth? Without me, you are a dead man. Together, we can expose them."

"Oh yeah, I'll add a great deal of credibility."

"I don't have a chance without you. They're too big."

"Sorry."

"You're all I've got."

"I've totally forgotten. Remind me why I care."

"You don't have a chance without me. You know that."

There was a long silence. Noah was about to hang up.

"Two things," she said. " Get out now. At 10 this morning, meet me at the end of the pier at Aquatic Park. If you're not there, you are either stupid or dead. In either case, you're not much use to me."

"Listen. . . ."

Click. She was quite clear. Noah had two choices. Believe her or not, it didn't matter. There was a Tiger behind both doors.

He splashed some water on his face, brushed his teeth and dressed quickly, placing the gun in his coat and heading out. He used the door that opened from the basement. No one could see it open from the street, and no one would be able to see Noah until he began climbing the concrete stairs up to the alley.

He glanced at his Alfa Romeo. No car, he decided. It was nearly six in the morning. He had four hours to make up his mind.

EIGHTEEN

RARELY UP THIS early, he noticed how — even before full light — the streets were alive. Commuters coming in from the East Bay filled the streets. Cabs, buses, delivery trucks, people in suits; all moving at the hurried pace of people who knew where they were going, the same places they went every morning and angry at anything that got in their paths — the "wait" sign, automobiles running the lights or turning in front of them, or other people. Many of them held large cups of caffeine, no doubt to cope.

It struck him that most of these people probably didn't even know their employers, didn't know their employer's employers.

He maneuvered downtown, toward the retail district. On Sutter he found a cheap diner and a stool. He unfolded the *Chronicle* as the woman brought the coffee and scribbled out the order. Three eggs scrambled. Whole Wheat Toast.

SUSPECTED KILLER SLAIN

Police are following up leads in yesterday's North Beach drive-by shooting. Franklin E. Hubbard, a suspected gun-for-hire was killed as he sat at a Columbus Street cafe. Frightened patrons of Rigoletto's scattered as a bullet fired from a passing gray sedan entered the skull of the 45 year-old suspected criminal.

Officials at the police department aren't speculating about the motive behind the shooting that took place at 10 a.m. on a street crowded with tourists and area residents. However, a source close to Homicide indicated that Hubbard was a suspect in the arson murder of young member of a Vietnamese gang.

Payback has not been ruled out, the source says. Witnesses could not identify the shooter. . . .

Noah was amazed at the slant of the story. Zip's death had nothing to do with Vietnamese gangs. The boy Zip murdered was a mistake. And in any event, the victim was Thanh's friend who worked in a restaurant at one of the hotels. Nothing illicit, according to Thanh, except that he occasionally dressed as a woman in his off hours.

According to the media, the missile hitting the truck was nothing more than the accidental ignition of illegal fireworks and now the hit on Hubbard was attributed to gang warfare. Noah never realized how little he knew, how little everyone knew, about how governments are run, about who has the power. It was easy to get squashed if you get in the way. Ask Thanh.

After three coffee refills, Noah continued his walk. He believed it was harder for anyone to tail him if he was walking. He stopped to look into store windows, detoured down to Post and then back up to Sutter. On Polk Street he meandered from a coffee shop where he ordered only juice and up the street to a news shop and thumbed through magazines, letting time force his decision, but all the while heading toward the meeting as if he would have it.

Finally, he boarded the Van Ness Bus and headed down to Fisherman's Wharf. Van Ness ended a few hundred yards before the pier began. There it was, stretched out before him, a spiraling jetty of concrete that halted out in the rough waters of the Bay. He saw the "Mascara" bobbing in the calmer inlet formed by the curve of the pier.

The Mascara was tied to the San Francisco Sea Scout Base. No doubt Olympia slipped into the city secretly on her floating "safe house" (as she called it), down through one of the tributaries feeding the bay, or from somewhere up or down the coast, coming in under the Golden Gate.

Once past the Scout Base, Noah was on the concrete pier — a huge and curving concrete slab, pockmarked from wear and neglect. It was odd that something so grand at a distance seemed so neglected and so deserted up close. The place seemed forlorn. A few fisherman hung poles over the wall. A lonely tourist idled further up.

The Golden Gate Bridge was to the left. The Bay Bridge was on his right. Piers with warehouses were on both sides. Nestled against the piers were docked vessels that looked no longer seaworthy. Alcatraz was straight ahead in the choppy water.

Noah stopped and looked back. Two, slightly concave high rises were behind him and to the left. A wooded hill was behind and to the right.

He kept walking, seeing a few tourists with cameras and a skater down at the far end, where Olympia, or an assassin probably waited. The sun was strong, but so was the chill in the wind, creating sensuous, countervailing sensations. He was sure the figure in the long coat way down at the rounded end of the pier was Olympia. Noah was especially alert as he began the trek on the jetty. Time seemed to move slower. Maybe it was just the pace of people not caught up in the work day, people relaxing, out for a smoke . . . time on their hands . . . out and away from the city . . . out here on the sea. He wasn't sure. There was a sense of the surreal. But there was nothing more than the calmness, the clarity of the sun in a cloudless sky.

She'd been smart. Maybe it was all right. Maybe this was the way it was all supposed to be. Maybe she was legit this time — unless she was going to do it herself. Unless she was going to kill him — a last and very intimate act. He couldn't imagine it. Things were going to be fine, he told himself.

If that was the case, why did he feel like something was going to happen. And that whatever it was, it wasn't good.

The end of the spiral seemed to be a secure place. In public, yet at a distance. Any drive-by would have to be by boat and there were foot-thick concrete walls to duck behind. Or by air. He looked up into the sky. Scanned the horizon. Saw nothing but birds.

Sounds picked up as he walked the long strip to her. Water lapping, sounds of a ship's horn in the distance, the harsh grind of a seaplane's engine, gulls calling.

She was without make up. Her hair was windblown. She was smiling. Relief? Hope? She seemed so much older. There was something genuine about her presence. Seemed as if a veil had been lifted. Seemed as if the games were over.

As he approached, she opened her bag.

"Nora?" Noah asked.

"You know Nora?" she asked, looking puzzled.

"Aren't you Nora?"

She started to speak, but didn't.

At the same time, her face froze. He heard a strange sound, a "thwop" and noticed something odd. A red spot appeared on her forehead. In the same instant, she tilted backward against the wall behind her and dropped limply like a Raggedy Ann doll tossed away by a bored child.

Suddenly the only sounds were the waves lapping and the gulls screeching.

Noah jerked back around. There was nothing. Two young German men were standing at the railing. They hadn't seen her fall. One youth was guiding another into the right pose for a photograph, hoping no doubt to get Alcatraz in the background.

A bicyclist was peddling toward them, leisurely. Fisherman fished. The Royal Prince, a ferryboat full of passengers on its decks, was gliding along nearby. Noah looked back to the city. Something ought to have changed. Nothing had. The only difference between this moment and the moment before was that Olympia was dead. Worse, he seemed to be the only one in this drama.

In the distance he saw the figures of two men in long coats coming his way. They didn't look to be tourists. A few feet more and he noticed suits beneath their raincoats. One was big and Caucasian. The other small and Black. They seemed to be in no hurry.

Noah, in disbelief, realized who they were.

"Who are you, the Grim Reaper?" Stern asked when he got there. And he got there in no particular hurry.

"Not how I had him pictured," Rose said. "Though he looks a bit grim at the moment. I don't think he's a reaper though."

"You sure?" Stern asked. "He seems to hang around with dead people a lot."

"You got a reaper's license?" Rose asked Noah, who didn't bother to answer. "Don't think he can reap. Never saw him actually reaping." Rose squatted beside Olympia.

Apparently sensing something, people began to wander close.

"Get away," Stern yelled at them. "We're trying to make a movie

141

here." Then to Rose, "Is she dead?"

Rose looked up. "She's giving a very convincing portrayal."

"How the hell?" Noah said, looking around, inviting them to look as well, see how impossible it was for her to have been shot.

"How in the hell what?" Stern asked.

"How did they get to her? From where?"

"Lang, you gotta keep up," Stern said. "A private dick — and we appreciate you keepin' it that way, don't we Rose? A private dick like you don't even know what's going on in this world. They got guns my boy, accurate at 2500 yards. That is, translated for your average Joe, 25 football fields end to end." Then to Rose as the detective stood. "Fifty caliber?"

Rose shrugged, then nodded.

"Man, these guys. . . ." Rose said, shaking his head. Noah couldn't tell if the expression was awe or disgust.

"What guys?" Noah asked.

"Just guys, you know," Stern said.

"No, I don't know," Noah shouted.

"You think he knows?" Stern asked Rose.

"Says he doesn't know. I don't know if he knows. Only he knows if he knows, you know?"

"Me, I'm Sergeant Schultz," Stern said. "I know nothing."

"How is it that you showed up here?" Noah asked.

"Everybody has to be somewhere, don't they?" Stern asked.

"If they're not somewhere else. Now me, I prefer to be where I am. And I'm here. And you're here."

"And you don't need to be here," Stern said to Noah.

"Aren't you going to ask me any questions?" Noah asked, incredulous.

"Okay," Stern said. "What's your favorite color?"

"No wait," Rose said. "If you were stranded on a deserted island. . . ."

"Jesus!" Noah said.

"Relax," Rose said, without the smartass tone. "Go home. They don't want you."

Stern pulled a cell phone from his inside pocket and punched in some numbers. Rose knelt again by the body, finding a small bag under

142

the crumpled body and began to examine its contents.

"Oh," Rose said, pulling a thick envelope from the purse. "Mr. Lang, this has your name on it." He handed the envelope to Noah. "Now get out of here."

Noah walked away. No one tried to stop him.

Walking back, Noah wondered how would they deal with the death, this woman with a hole in her head — Rawley's wife, Olympia or Nora or whoever this woman was, whose body lay crumpled at the end of Aquatic Pier, whoever this woman was, whose spirit was released in the final curl of the spiraling jetty.

"Goodbye Olympia," he said.

He passed the "Mascara," as it rose and fell ever so slightly upon the water. The old man who she said was her father was now out on the deck, sitting on the side, gathering a bit of cold sun while he waited for his passenger.

"They don't want you," he remembered Rose saying. The thought made him feel especially inconsequential. He had never mattered in the grand scheme of things. Who did?

Noah was back at his office building before noon and ran into Brinkman outside, heading out for lunch.

"The boys told me someone put a hit out on the hitman," Brinkman said, smiling.

"That right?" Noah said.

"They say some Vietnamese gang. That's just for the press, you know?"

"Oh?"

"Knew too much."

"As good a reason as any."

"So Noah, looks like you're in the clear."

"That's what I'm told."

Brinkman gave him an odd smile in return. A strange smile. It wasn't friendly. A knowing smile, perhaps.

Thanh faced the window. He turned as Noah entered.

"The lock doesn't work," Thanh said, referring to the door.

"Good."

143

"I brought Latte." Thanh gestured toward the two cups on the desk, both still with lids. "That was hours ago."

"I'm sorry. I was . . . out."

"I didn't know where else to go. I'm a little confused, I think." Thanh looked as if he'd been crying.

"You don't have a corner on the market," Noah said.

Thanh nodded, smiled. But it looked like he was going to cry.

"You ever going to get a microwave?" Thanh asked.

"Maybe."